"Move in h

When Elyn didn't ~~reply,~~
"You can leave your hotel and move in here to
look after me."

"M-move in here?" she finally exclaimed, staring
at him thunderstruck, her heartbeat racing at
just that very thought. "I'm not doing anything
of the kind!"

"You don't think you owe me something?"

"Not *that* much!" Elyn retorted.

"Even though it's your fault that I can't look
after myself?" Max's tone was challenging and
Elyn found her resolve was weakening.

Jessica Steele first tried her hand at writing romance novels at her husband's encouragement two years after they were married. She fondly remembers the day her first novel was accepted for publication. "Peter mopped me up, and neither of us cooked that night," she recalls. "We went out to dinner." She and her husband live in a hundred-year-old cottage in Worcestershire, and they've traveled to many fascinating places—including China, Japan, Mexico and Hungary—that make wonderful settings for her books.

Books by Jessica Steele

ITALIAN INVADER
Jessica Steele

Harlequin Books

TORONTO • NEW YORK • LONDON
AMSTERDAM • PARIS • SYDNEY • HAMBURG
STOCKHOLM • ATHENS • TOKYO • MILAN
MADRID • WARSAW • BUDAPEST • AUCKLAND

ISBN 0-373-03327-3

ITALIAN INVADER

Copyright © 1993 by Jessica Steele.

Printed in U.S.A.

CHAPTER ONE

ELYN gripped the telephone and waited anxiously while the hotel telephonist rang her mother and stepfather's room.

'I'm sorry,' the telephonist came back on the line to inform her, 'they're not answering. Would you like to leave a message? I can have it sent to their room for their return.'

The woman's tone was pleasant, and somehow Elyn managed to hold down her rising sense of panic. 'My name is Elyn Talbot. Would you ask either of them to ring me, as a matter of some urgency, please,' she requested, finding an equally pleasant tone.

She replaced the phone, owning that, although she had always thought herself level-headed and not given to panicking, she was on the verge of panicking now.

She glanced at the pages of figures she had just re-checked for the umpteenth time, and suddenly felt the need to clear her head. She knew, as she slipped the pages of figure-work into her desk drawer and locked it, that things could not be worse. So it was with a vain hope that perhaps matters would not look so terrifyingly black when she returned that she shrugged into her coat, and decided to take herself off for a walk.

First, though, the need to share the dreadfulness of her knowledge took her in the direction of the design department where her gifted stepbrother worked. Not that Guy would be able to help in any way, but it was such a frightening burden to carry alone.

Had Samuel Pillinger, her stepfather and owner of Pillinger Ceramics, been anywhere around she would at once have gone to him to report that it did not look as if they'd be able to pay the staff wages at the end of the month, let alone their suppliers. But he wasn't around. Even after she had warned him, yet again, how bad things were, he had still carried out his promise to take her mother to London for a few days' break.

Break! They were broke, Elyn thought humourlessly, and turned the handle of the design section door and went in. 'Guy not around?' she asked Hugh Burrell, a man she had no liking for, albeit that he was quite good at his job.

Hugh Burrell didn't like her either, she knew that. He had taken a dislike to her ever since that day a couple of years ago when he'd asked her out and she'd declined. Stuck-up, he'd called her. But it wasn't that she was stuck-up, but that, apart from the fact that there was something about the sly-eyed look of him she couldn't take to, she made it a rule never to date anyone from work. She had done so once, only to discover afterwards that the man thought that entitled him to special privileges at work.

'He's at the dentist,' Hugh Burrell answered, his foxy eyes making a meal of her long honey-blonde hair and trim figure.

'Thanks,' she murmured, and realising that she was so worried that she had forgotten Guy had said at breakfast that he'd a dental appointment this morning, Hugh Burrell's stare was making her flesh creep, and she walked out.

Ten minutes later, having made it to the parkland side of Bovington, she slowed her pace and, despite its being a cold October day, she sank down on to one of the wooden benches scattered about—and felt not one whit better for her ten-minute walk.

Worried she fretted again and again on how, from the beginning of the year, she had tried to warn Sam Pillinger about exactly how bad things were getting. But, like his son, more artist than academic, he'd either not believed things were as desperate as she said, or had decided, like Mr Micawber, that something would turn up.

But nothing had turned up. Though, when Elyn had insisted on going through last month's figures with him, she had thought she was finally beginning to get through. 'As bad as that, eh!' he had commented, chewing thoughtfully on his pipe. But, when Elyn had been hoping he might add something constructive about how they were going to survive should the rumours be true that one of their chief outlets was going bust, all she got was his opinion that the rumours were just scaremongering. To which he had added a few bitter comments on how he blamed any failing of his own business on the newcomer, Maximilian Zappelli.

In point of fact, Elyn recalled, Maximilian Zappelli had taken over the ailing firm of Gradburns in the next town of Pinwich about two years ago—and promptly started to make it profitable! Signor Zappelli already had an extremely prosperous business in marble and mosaics in Italy, so Elyn realised he must have deemed that to have a ceramics connection in England would be a sound business move. In the process of making Gradburns a going concern, however, he had taken quite a chunk of Pillingers' trade and, with Pinwich not ten miles away from Bovington, quite a few of their highly specialised staff too.

That in itself, Elyn felt, was reason enough not to like him. After all, Pillingers had trained them—and he had poached them.

A strand of fairness gave her a nudge to suggest that, since Maximilian Zappelli spent more time in Italy than he did in England, it was probable his manager was the one who had poached some of their key workers.

Seated on her bench, she sank her hands into her pockets in an irritated gesture, her beautiful green eyes staring unseeingly in front of her. That still didn't mean

that she liked Maximilian Zappelli any better! Not that
she'd ever met him—or wanted to! But she knew his
type. He'd been in the papers again only the other day.
For an Italian, said to be living for the most part in Italy,
he certainly had his share of publicity in the British Press,
she thought sourly.

He hadn't been alone, she recalled without effort. But
then he never was! As if the picture was still in front of
her she again saw the tall, dark-haired, evening-suited
mid-thirties male with an elegant and beautiful female
on his arm. Naturally he'd be squiring some woman
around, and naturally she'd be beautiful—and naturally, she'd be a different female from the one he'd hit
the headlines with the last time.

Men like him—philanderer, Elyn had dubbed him—
made her cross. The worst of it was that women fell for
that sort of man in droves. She had no need to look
further than her stepsister Loraine to know that.

Not that Loraine had ever met Maximilian Zappelli
either, but Loraine seemed to have an inbuilt penchant
for the Casanova type and lurched from one disastrous
relationship to another.

Strangely though, Elyn mused, considering her mother
had been through the same ghastly experience at the
hands of a womaniser, she seemed to have little sym-
pathy for her stepdaughter. Nor did Sam Pillinger seem
to be able to cope with having his much indulged
daughter weeping about the place. So it was left to Elyn
to cope when Loraine wailed, 'But I thought he loved
me,' and Elyn it was who soothed and sympathised—
until Loraine was ready to pitch headlong into her next
disaster. There was nothing Elyn could do but watch.
But she knew the philandering type! And hated them!
Never would she have any truck with a man of that sort.
Her own father had been the same—all charm and
no substance.

Elyn remembered her childhood as being a most bewildering time. She had been a quiet and sensitive child who loved both her parents, but who shrank into herself at the violence of their arguments. For either her parents were all in all to each other, or there would be raised voices with crockery flying. She remembered frequent other times seeing her mother distressed and alone when Jack Talbot would go off for weeks at a time—and recalled yet more rows, more tears and recriminations when, as always, he came back. Loving her father as she did, it had been painful to learn at an early age that life was much more peaceful when he was not at home.

She had been twelve years old when her father had again done a disappearing trick. It was the last time. Ann Talbot had divorced him, and Elyn, keeping her hurt to herself, had not seen him since.

Only much later had she learned of the many affairs her mother had forgiven him, of the many times she had believed in his protestations of love and how it would never happen again—until, after one affair too many, she had finally thrown in the towel.

Her mother had been working part-time then at Pillingers, the ceramic art manufacturers, and they had gone through an alarming period when her suspicion that maintenance due from her ex-husband would never materialise became fact. For an age they had gone through an absolutely dreadful and frightening time of scraping along to try and keep ahead of the bills, and never quite making it. They were still owing money when Ann Talbot managed to switch to a full-time vacancy at Pillingers, and she had continued to struggle to pay off their debts.

Things had started to look up, however, when some while later her mother introduced her to her employer, the widowed Samuel Pillinger, and shortly after that asked her how she'd feel about having him for a stepfather.

'You're going to marry him?' Elyn had asked, wide-eyed, going on fifteen and romantic. 'You're in love with him?'

'I've had love—you can keep it,' her mother had replied coldly. 'Sam Pillinger's about the best bargain going, and it's time I looked after number one.'

Elyn supposed she couldn't blame her mother that she had toughened up a little since, dewy-eyed, she had gone into her first marriage, so she suppressed her shock and told her mother, 'I want you to be happy.'

'I will be,' her mother had declared firmly.

A month later Ann had married her employer, and she and Elyn had moved out of their rented accommodation and into the large and rambling lovely old house where Samuel Pillinger lived with his fifteen-year-old son and seventeen-year-old daughter and Mrs Munslow, their housekeeper.

Although the new Mrs Pillinger gave up her job, she saw no reason whatsoever to dispense with Madge Munslow's services, and in no time life at the Grange had settled down very pleasantly.

Elyn liked both her stepsister Loraine and her stepbrother Guy, and swiftly took to Mrs Munslow. Though it was Guy, a quiet and shy boy, with whom she spent most time. Loraine was finding the company of the opposite sex of much more interest than a pair of fifteen-year-olds.

In the next year Elyn grew fond of her new family, discovering her stepfather to be a kind man who, to her great relief, was true to his wife. A man who said little and believed in the work ethic.

That belief, however, did not extend to cover his daughter. Loraine was clearly his favourite, and was able to twist him around her little finger—she got away with murder! Loraine decided at sixteen that she'd had enough of school, and left. She decided, too, that she didn't want a job or career—and, with her father happy to give her a generous allowance, did not seek one.

It was different for Elyn and Guy, though. When they were sixteen and thinking about careers, it was Samuel Pillinger's view that they should forget about any further education nonsense and start building a career in the ceramic art world.

'You want us to start work at the studios?' Guy had asked.

'Why not?' his father had responded. 'It'll be yours one day, yours and Loraine's. Elyn will have a stake in it too.' He smiled in her direction. 'Now, what I suggest is that you go through each department in turn, and . . .'

That conversation had taken place six years ago, Elyn reflected as she glanced at her watch and realised, just in case Sam and her mother had returned to their hotel and had been trying to contact her, that she'd better go back to her office.

They had, for the most part, been six happy years, she recalled as she headed back the way she had come. She and Guy had spent six months in each of the departments, from slip-room through moulding and modelling, firing and decorating, not forgetting the administration side of the business. Elyn had an outstanding ability where figures were concerned, and it was in that section that she shone.

'Why, you're brilliant!' her stepfather had exclaimed when in no time she had caught up on his backlog of confidential paperwork. And from that day he had left her to take care of anything confidential and to learn all she could of office procedures, and gone back to spend a large slice of his time in his beloved design section where, this being an area where his son shone, he had set about teaching him all he knew.

As year by year someone either retired or left to work elsewhere, so gradually, and by dint of dedicated effort, Elyn worked her way to the top. She had owned to feeling a little startled at waking up one morning the previous year to realise that, at twenty-one, she was the one ultimately in charge of everything relating to administration.

She re-entered the gates of Pillingers and realised that, if her calculations were correct, there would be nothing for her to be in charge of! Sorely did she wish she had made a miscalculation somewhere—but she knew she hadn't.

She decided against going to seek Guy out again. It was seldom that she went to the design section, and if anyone had heard a whisper about Huttons, their main outlet, going broke, then, knowing how rumours spread from department to department like wildfire, she didn't want any speculative rumour starting up that she had urgently been trying to get in touch with the owner's son.

Back in her office, her first action was to pick up the phone. 'Any calls for me, Rachel? I had to pop out for a while.'

'No, none,' Rachel answered.

'Thanks. Oh, can you give me an outside line?' Elyn asked, as though she'd only then remembered that she wanted to make a call.

A minute later and Elyn was asking the hotel telephonist if either Mr or Mrs Samuel Pillinger was available.

'Just one moment, please,' the telephonist replied politely—and Elyn waited.

She waited quite some while, but only realised just how anxious and upset she was when she heard her stepfather answer, 'Hello?' and felt she could have easily burst into tears.

'Sam, it's me, Elyn.'

'Hello, love. Just been reading a message from you. You're lucky you've caught us. We only came back because your mother wanted to change her shoes. She...'

'Sam, listen to me—it's urgent,' Elyn cut him off—if her mother's feet were suffering from doing too much sightseeing then she couldn't feel a hundred per cent sympathetic right now.

'I'm listening,' he invited.

Elyn took a deep breath, and while knowing that no one could possibly overhear, she stated quietly, 'Keith Ipsley rang me this morning...' She paused as she took another steadying breath. 'Huttons have folded.'

'Folded! Gone bust, you mean?'

'That's what I mean,' she replied as evenly as she could.

'But—but, we were expecting a cheque from them—— My stars, they owe us thousands!'

'I know. Which is why I rang them as soon as I got the tip-off. I'm sorry, Sam,' she had to tell him reluctantly, 'they've got the receivers in. We'll be lucky if we get ten pence in the pound, and lord knows how long we'll have to wait for that.'

It took him but seconds to digest what she had said, then he said what she'd been hoping he would say. 'I'd better come home,' he stated flatly, and as Elyn guessed her mother hadn't liked the sound of that and had made some sound to remind him of her presence. 'Er—do you want a word with Ann?'

'Not right now,' Elyn said gently, and said goodbye, to put down the phone knowing that, love her parent though she might, things were so grave at the Bovington end, she hadn't the heart for idle chit-chat.

Elyn tried to immerse herself in some work in the following hours, but her thoughts kept returning again and again to the knock on effect of Huttons' calling in the official receiver. Part of the amount outstanding from Huttons had been promised without fail for this week, and was needed. She supposed she should be grateful that Keith Ipsley, Huttons' chief clerk, had felt so personally responsible that he couldn't keep his word about that cheque that he'd had the decency to tip her off.

Not that she could blame him about his broken promise over the cheque. It wasn't his fault that his firm had gone under. Poor man, things weren't very rosy for him either. From yesterday being chief clerk at the reputable firm of Huttons, he was, from that morning, like the rest of the Huttons payroll, without a job.

When the stark reality hit her that she too, not to mention the rest of the Pillinger workforce, would be without a job unless by some miracle Sam could see a way out that she couldn't, Elyn loaded her briefcase and went home. Knowing what she knew, she would have a hard time looking the tea girl in the eye, let alone anyone else.

She guessed that Sam would drop her mother off first, but there was no sign of his car on the drive. Elyn went to the kitchen where the big motherly-looking woman she had gown so fond of stood with her hands up to her elbows in flour.

'What are you doing home?' Madge Munslow looked up in surprise, a special smile of warmth on her mouth for the mistress's daughter.

'Playing truant,' Elyn returned her smile, while a sick feeling hit her stomach as it dawned on her that there was every possibility that they wouldn't be able to afford Madge for much longer. Oh, dear lord, Madge was past sixty, and now had extra help in the house, but who would take her on if they had to let her go? 'In case neither my mother nor Mr Pillinger have phoned, they're coming back some time today, not tomorrow, as planned,' Elyn told her in a rush.

'Well, I'm glad somebody thought to let me know there'll be two extra for dinner,' Madge grumbled good-naturedly. 'Want a cup of tea, Elyn?' she asked.

But suddenly Elyn was finding that she couldn't look the housekeeper in the eye either, and, doing a swift about-turn, she waved her briefcase and said, 'Can't stop, I've some paperwork I want to go through.'

In her room Elyn exchanged her smart office suit for shirt and trousers and a light sweater, but, unable to settle to anything, she went to stand at her bedroom window. The house was set in its own grounds, but Elyn saw neither the well manicured lawns nor the avenue of beautiful trees. Her attention was rigidly on the drive, as she watched for her stepfather's return.

In actual fact, though, it was Guy who returned first. She saw his car headlights, saw him pull round and on to the standing area, and, just in case he'd any plans to go out that night, she hurried down the stairs to meet him.

'You're in first—that's unusual,' he commented in friendly fashion when he saw her.

'How was the dentist?' she just remembered to ask.

'Barbaric! You look worried,' he said, coming closer. 'What's up?'

'Huttons have the official receiver in.'

'No!'

'Straight up,' she told him.

'Strewth!' he gasped. Then, 'How will that affect us?'

There was no way of dressing it up, though he'd have had to have his head well and truly buried in the sand to have not heard something of the discussions she'd had at home with his father. 'Badly,' she replied bleakly. 'Are you going out tonight?'

'I was, but...'

'I've contacted Sam, he and my mother will be here soon, I expect.'

'Things must be bad if the old man's agreed to cut short his break,' Guy opined.

'Can you stay in? It—er—might affect you more than any of us,' Elyn suddenly realised, and saw, as Guy suddenly looked serious, that it had just dawned on him too that the ceramic art studios he had been led to believe he might one day part-own might not be his after all.

'I think I'd better,' he agreed anxiously.

Both she and Guy were downstairs in the hall when an hour later the solid front door again opened and Ann and Samuel Pillinger came in.

'Get Madge to bring some tea into the drawing-room in ten minutes; we'll talk in there,' Samuel decided, as he and his wife went up the elegant staircase to freshen up.

'They're home,' Elyn told Madge, but made the tea herself, and put four cups and saucers on a tray.

'And thirsty, by the look of it,' Madge quipped—and Elyn couldn't bear to think of her home without her.

It was fifteen minutes before they were all assembled in the drawing-room. Elyn hadn't thought for a moment that her mother would not be there, since she must be aware that her financial security was sounding shaky. Which was fine by her, but Elyn was quite relieved that her stepsister was at present away visiting friends. She was fond of Loraine, but felt that there were far more serious matters to deal with here than to have Loraine throw a fit if, as seemed likely, her allowance came under threat. Time to deal with that later.

'I've checked,' Samuel Pillinger opened, 'and there's no mistake. Huttons have gone under—taking our money with them.' His solemn glance went to his wife, then to his son, and finally settled on his stepdaughter. 'How do we stand, Elyn?' he asked quietly.

Elyn cleared her throat. 'We don't,' she answered huskily.

'We fall?'

'I'm afraid so,' she agreed miserably, and, reaching for her briefcase, she got out figures which she had checked so frequently she knew them by heart. 'I wish it were different, but it isn't, and no amount of wishing can alter the fact that we can't pay the staff wages, let alone our other commitments.'

'It *can't* be as bad as that!' Guy broke in to protest.

'If Elyn says it is, then it must be,' stated his father. 'Let's have a look at your figures, Elyn.'

A full half-hour went by with the atmosphere in the room going from serious to gloomy to downright dejection. Though at the end of that half-hour they were all agreed, her mother included, that whatever else happened, the staff wages were top priority.

'By tomorrow word will have got out about Huttons— you can't keep a thing like that quiet,' Sam declared. 'But as yet no one knows the extent of credit we allowed them or the disastrous effect their going to the wall has had on us. I'm afraid, Guy, that you'll have to go in to work tomorrow as if nothing has happened, while Elyn and I visit the bank, and solicitors, and anybody else I can think of who might give us a chance of clawing our way out of this damned hole.'

Up until then Ann Pillinger had stayed silent, but, as Elyn glanced over to where her mother was seated taking everything in, she was startled by the harshness of her expression and the vehemence of her words as she erupted suddenly, 'It's that damned Italian's fault! If that Zappelli man hadn't pushed in and bought out Gradburns, we'd never be in this fix!'

Again Elyn's innate sense of fairness struggled to the surface. While she held no brief for the wretched continental philanderer, she didn't think in all honesty that he had 'pushed' in. So far as she was aware, no one else had made a bid, and Gradburns, so she'd heard, had snatched at his offer.

Though before she could give voice to her thoughts, Sam Pillinger was already agreeing with his wife. 'You're right, my dear. Damned interloper!' he muttered feelingly.

'But...' Elyn didn't get very far before, to her surprise, her stepbrother chipped in.

'He took some of our best staff too!' he complained acrimoniously.

'And our best customers...' Sam joined in, and for the next ten minutes, while Elyn stayed silent, the other three resentfully took Maximilian Zappelli apart.

When later that night in bed she was visited by a wisp of something akin to guilt because she had not once spoken up in honest defence of the man, Elyn dismissed that wisp of guilt out of hand. Speak up for him, for goodness' sake? Her thoughts flitted back to the dreadful predicament Pillingers were in—and devil take it, she fumed, her family were right! Why on earth should she defend the womanising Latin!

Thoughts of Maximilian Zappelli were far from her mind the following morning. Mr Eldred, the bank manager, had heard of Huttons' demise, and wasn't at all happy about her stepfather's bright idea of increasing their overdraft.

'Then how am I going to pay the staff their wages at the end of the month? Tell me that?' Samuel demanded.

'You have three weeks until then. Might I suggest you take a look at your share portfolio?' Mr Eldred hinted.

'Sell my shares?'

They came away from the bank with Sam Pillinger muttering darkly about having done business with that particular bank for donkey's years, but where were they when you really needed them.

A man of honour, he considered that the wages bill should have top priority, and had given instructions that his shares should go. But as the week went on, the situation became totally hopeless when other suppliers of Huttons, who were still reeling from the shock of knowing that they were not going to be paid, refused to supply Pillingers until their outstanding accounts were settled.

The writing had already been on the wall, but, having made a valiant effort to keep his company, Samuel at last had to admit defeat. But it was an honourable defeat in that when, on the last day of October, the firm closed down, having sold everything he possibly could sell at short notice but without a penny to call his own, he had managed to avoid bankruptcy, and owed no one.

'I'm so sorry,' Elyn murmured gently as she stood with him and Guy saying goodbye to each member of their workforce in turn as they filed by.

'Me too, Dad,' said Guy, in the lull. 'What's to do now?' he asked, and although Elyn herself had been wondering the same, she was still staggered by his reply.

For, 'Have a bit of a rest, then start up again,' she distinctly heard his father reply.

'Start up again!' she exclaimed, and as both father and son stared at her, 'We haven't the money, Sam, to start up anything!' She tried to make him see. 'We don't have any money to live on, to...' She broke off, re-alising that, artist that he was, artist that his son was, neither of them, even now, had fully grasped the reality of the situation. She tried another tack. 'I rather thought that, having sold all the movable equipment here, you—er—might be thinking in terms of selling the kilns, the buildings, the...'

'What?' he exclaimed, astonished. 'Sell—for the Italian to buy! *Never!*'

As far as Elyn was aware, Maximilian Zappelli wasn't remotely interested in the Pillinger building. Though rather than provoke Sam by saying as much, when none but the most insensitive must see what a painful day this must be for him, she stayed quiet while he went on, 'My father started this firm—I'll get it going again, just see if I don't!'

The subject was dropped when Hugh Burrell came into view. Sam held out his hand, his little speech of regret at the ready. But his hand was ignored, as he was ignored, as Guy too was ignored. Hugh Burrell did stop in front of Elyn, however, his sly eyes giving her the once-over. 'Thanks for the Christmas present!' he said nastily and, while it registered with Elyn that losing his job so close to Christmas hadn't made him any nicer a person, it also registered that this man resented her—and bore her a grudge. She was glad she would never have to see him again.

It was a sad day for all three of them, but eventually they locked up the building and went home. They went in their separate cars, but arrived at the house in convoy.

'Was it so bad?' she heard her mother gently greet Sam, and felt proud of her parent that, unlike his daughter, she was being far more supportive now the blow had actually fallen than she had at first shown.

'I need a stiff drink,' she heard him reply—and saw a sulky-looking Loraine, who had been told her allowance wouldn't be there in the bank on the first of the month as usual, came out into the hall.

'And I desperately need a little money, Daddy,' she told him soulfully.

At once Ann Pillinger's gentle tone fell away. 'Then get yourself a job, and start earning some!' she slammed at her.

'*Daddy*!' Loraine wailed—but, perhaps for the first time in his life, Sam didn't seem to hear her, and went into the drawing-room with his wife.

The idea of finding herself a job was ever present in Elyn's mind, even if her stepsister had no such intention. The thought of debt began to prey on her mind, but, scan the papers though she might, Elyn saw nothing locally that paid very much. She did spot a couple of jobs in London which she could do, and which paid extremely well. But, since her aim was to earn enough to be able to put something into the family coffers, it would be defeating the object if she worked away from home and had to pay out half her income on rent and living expenses in London.

Her best talent lay in administration, she recognised that, but such jobs, in either Bovington or Pinwich, were few and far between. She took to looking for jobs in any other field, but anything unskilled paid unskilled wages.

As yet none of them had had the heart to tell Madge Munslow that they could not afford to keep her, and, as November began to draw to a close and, beside an assortment of bills arriving, another pay-day for the housekeeper loomed, Elyn started to feel desperate.

If the rest of the family were busy looking for paid work she would be surprised. But with Guy seeming to adopt his father's 'something will turn up' attitude, and Loraine—between loves at the moment—mooning about the place, and Elyn's own mother seeming to have joined the 'something will turn up' brigade too, Elyn was starting to get quite cross with the lot of them. That afternoon she went out and sold her car.

'What on earth did you do that for?' was the astonished reception that news brought over the dinner-table.

'Because Madge will need paying in a few days' time, and a few other day-to-day running costs will require paying too,' she answered.

'I didn't ask you to sell your car!' Sam declared proudly, and all at once Elyn wasn't cross any more, but upset that she had hurt his pride.

'I know you didn't, Sam,' she assured him gently. 'Just as I didn't ask you to buy me that car for my eighteenth birthday—but you did. Anyhow,' she found a light note to tease, 'I'm sure one of the first things you'll do when you're on your feet again will be to buy me another one!'

That crisis of bruised feelings passed, but as November gave way to December Elyn started to grow desperate again. She had got a good price for her car, but with that money being the only money available among all of them, it was going down at an alarming rate.

Elyn was in a desperate frame of mind when a day or so later, as she scanned the early afternoon edition of the local paper, she saw a job that not only paid well but was within daily travelling distance. Her initial reaction on seeing who the firm was, though, who were advertising for someone to take charge of a statistics section, was to quickly go on to the next advert. But, having scanned every other ad in the situations vacant column without seeing a thing that paid remotely as well, nor sounded half as interesting, she glanced back again, and again, to the advert.

Her family would go mad if she so much as applied, much less was successful and actually got the job. But the money was excellent, and—she nibbled anxiously at her lower lip—money was what they needed, quite frantically—and nobody else was bringing any in.

But I'm not a statistician! She started to get cold feet, and talk herself out of it. Nonsense, said an inner female that was made of sterner stuff, she was highly numerate and could read a balance sheet as easily as she could read a novel—so what was difficult about statistics?

On that note of bravado she grabbed up the phone in her room and quickly dialled the number, and as a voice said, 'Good afternoon, Zappelli Fine China,' she felt as if the words were screaming through the whole house.

Feeling like the worst kind of traitor, Elyn stamped down hard on such feelings. They needed money! For goodness' sake, get on with it. 'Good afternoon. Personnel, please,' she requested.

As simply as that she was put through and, having stated her business, in next to no time was sitting staring at the phone back on its cradle. She had an interview at eleven o'clock tomorrow morning! She had an interview at Zappelli's!

It had fully been her intention to acquaint her family with what she had done at dinner that evening. And indeed, she opened her mouth several times to do just that, but each time her courage failed her. There'd be hell to pay, she knew that, and she suddenly decided that, since her paper qualifications for the job were next to non-existent, there was every likelihood that she wouldn't get the job, so there was no point in upsetting everyone needlessly.

Calling herself a coward, she later went upstairs to her room, having half decided that, since she was more certain *not* to get the job than to get it, she wouldn't turn up for interview in the morning after all.

She did, of course. It seemed like a point of honour somehow that, having made the appointment, she should go through with it. Dressed in one of her good business suits, she let herself out of the house at ten o'clock the following morning. It took her fifteen minutes to walk to the railway station, and, after a wait of ten minutes, she caught the train which would put her down at the next stop. She alighted ten minutes later in the town of Pinwich.

Zappelli Fine China was a further ten minutes' walk away from the centre of town, but she was in plenty of time, and had no need to hurry.

She arrived to keep her appointment with a Mr Christopher Nickson with five minutes to spare, and was not kept waiting more than a few minutes beyond the appointed time. 'So sorry to keep you waiting, Miss Talbot,' the young man apologised pleasantly, clearly liking what he saw as he escorted her to his office. 'Now,' he began once they were seated, 'are you currently employed?'

One of Elyn's earlier causes for a feeling of discomfort had been that once they knew that she had anything to do with Pillingers the interview would stop there, but there was no way of avoiding it. 'I worked for Pillingers,' she began. 'Mr Pillinger is...'

'Ah yes, one or two of the Pillinger people have started here,' he interrupted with a smile as he confided, 'I moved up from Devon last month, and only started here myself on the first of December.'

From then on Elyn started to relax. Since he was not a local man—and since Talbot was a common enough name, so clearly he did not know of her connection with Pillingers—if things went badly—and suddenly she started to want as well as need the job—then neither he nor anyone else would be any the wiser.

'Now——' he resumed, and went on to give her more details of the job, and to ask if the job still appealed and if she thought she could do it.

'Yes, on both counts,' she told him, truly seeing nothing difficult in the work he had outlined, and the mathematically inclined part of her raring to have a crack at it.

'Great,' he smiled, and, picking up a pencil, 'If you could just give me a list of your qualifications—just for the record, then...' He looked up and broke off. 'Is something wrong?' he enquired.

'I don't have any qualifications,' Elyn had to confess, adding quickly lest he should terminate the interview there and then, 'But I know figures. I'm good at them!' This was no time for false modesty. 'If you'd like to give me an aptitude test or something of that sort, I'm sure I could prove that.'

She caught the train back to Bovington knowing that Christopher Nickson had been delighted with the results of the test which, after about half an hour of scurrying around, someone had worked out to give her. His promise to be in touch though, had left her not knowing whether she had the job or not.

For that reason, and believing that if they did have an applicant with paper qualifications she could say

goodbye to the job, Elyn decided against saying anything to her family about having gone for the interview.
There now seemed little point in needlessly causing a
family upset.

Trusting that Christopher Nickson would be in touch
as he had promised, be it only to say she had not been
successful at interview, she stayed near to the telephone
over the next couple of days. If anyone was going to
ring announcing themselves as 'Zappelli Fine China
here', then she wanted to be sure that she was the one
who took the call.

Even though her hopes had started to fade, she was
all set to stay near the phone on the third day too. But
as her stepfather ambled into the breakfast-room sifting
through the morning's post he'd picked up from the hall
en route, she was suddenly made startlingly aware that
Zappelli Fine China were not going to telephone. Because
suddenly her stepfather had halted stock-still and after
studying the top envelope in his hands, he looked straight
at her and demanded fiercely, 'What the hell are
Zappelli's writing to you for?'

Oh, dear, she thought, her stomach churning, and as
her stepfather came and thrust the envelope at her she
saw that the postage frank was emblazoned 'Zappelli
Fine China'. This was something she hadn't thought of.
'I—er—hmm,' she coughed, 'I—um—applied for a job
there.'

'You did *what*?'

'Well, I probably didn't get it,' she offered lamely.

'*Really*, Elyn!' her mother exploded.

'That's *loyalty*!' grunted Guy, and, with the exception
of Loraine who wasn't down yet, the family en masse
fell about her head.

She had known there would be a row, to put it mildly,
and for five minutes she put up with one after the other
going for her. But then *she* started to get annoyed. 'It's
all right for you to go on, Mother,' she cut her parent

off in the middle of her what-an-ungrateful-creature-you-are monologue, 'and I'm sorry I've had to do what I've done, but we can't just sit here forever waiting for something to turn up. Bills have to be paid somehow, and I just can't sit around adding to that debt without trying to do something about it. I know Zappelli is a dirty word, but their money's clean and they pay well. And,' she went on quickly when it looked as if her stepfather might erupt again, 'as I said, I probably didn't get the job anyway.'

'Perhaps you'd like to read your letter and let us know, so we can all wave a flag,' Ann Pillinger sniffed sarcastically.

Without enthusiasm, Elyn slit the envelope. Only then did she realise how very much she wanted the job. But as she unfolded the single sheet of paper and discovered that she had indeed got it, she felt none of the elation she might earlier have felt.

'I start on the second of January,' she stated flatly.

Her stepfather ignored her completely. 'Would you pass the toast, Ann?' he requested.

Elyn loved her family—but damn the lot of them, she fumed when fifteen minutes later she took herself off for a walk. It was like a funeral parlour back at the house. Heavens, you'd have thought she'd committed some cardinal sin!

She wouldn't have been at all surprised to have seen the curtains drawn, the house in mourning, when she returned an hour later. She supposed she'd better go in and make her peace.

Her stepfather was just coming out as she went in, and to her horror it seemed as though he intended to walk by her without a word, ignore her! 'Still hate me?' she asked him in a rush.

He stopped, paused, then looked her straight in the eye. She bore his look without flinching. 'Are you going to take that job?' he asked.

Steadily, she looked back, 'Yes,' she replied quietly, 'I am.'

She waited, fully expecting him to retort something pithy, but somehow she just couldn't back down. It might seem a crime in his eyes, but they *needed* the money. But then, to her relief, 'Who could hate you?' he grunted gruffly. 'Your motives are the best, I know that.'

'Oh, Sam!' she cried, and hugged him, and felt so much better when he hugged her back before he went meandering on his way.

Christmas passed quietly, with her mother thawing to her just a little, but with her stepbrother still very put out because she was joining a firm who he bitterly believed had played a major part in the demise of a firm that one day would have been his.

Elyn spent some of January the first, the national holiday, in pressing some of her good quality working suits, and in generally checking her wardrobe and making sure she had everything ready for the morrow.

She had not expected anyone to wish her luck the next morning, nor did they, but as she got up from the breakfast table, to her pleasure and surprise, she heard her mother say, 'Elyn, I'll run you to the station if you like.'

'Thanks,' she accepted readily, eager to put an end to the cold war. She felt better than ever when at the station before she got out of the car, her mother, never a very demonstrative person these days, leaned over and kissed her cheek. Elyn knew it was not a kiss in parting, but more a kiss of forgiveness.

On that cheerful note she made her way to Zappelli Fine China. Her work team were a couple of people round about her own age. Diana Kerr was a plain but pleasant young woman, and Neil Jennings was a thin young man, with a love, it soon transpired, of potholing.

Elyn was used to having loads of responsibility and fell into the role of head of department quite naturally, and in no time at all the three were working together harmoniously.

When at around eleven that morning the phone on her desk rang, Elyn stretched out her hand automatically without taking her eyes off her work. Given that it was new surroundings, it was as if she had never been away.

'Elyn, it's Chris, Chris Nickson,' he announced. 'How are you settling in?'

'Settled already is the answer to that, I think,' she smiled down the phone.

'Good. I should be free in about ten minutes. I thought it might be an idea if I took you on a tour of the place. How does that sound?'

'I'll look forward to it,' she told him, and replaced her phone feeling that it would make for more efficient management if she knew just where in the vast building each department lay.

True to his word, Chris Nickson arrived ten minutes later, and they left the office she shared with the two others, and he took her around to introduce her to the heads of the other departments.

In view of his remark at her interview about one or two of the Pillinger people starting there, Elyn fully expected to bump into at least a few of the people she knew. That she did not, however, was soon explained when Chris informed her, 'We haven't got a full workforce in today. A good few of them applied for an extra day's holiday. In view of the hours they put in when we have a rush order, Mr Orford, the manager,' he explained, 'was pleased to meet them halfway.'

'I see,' Elyn smiled, unable to remember the last time Pillingers had had a rush order. But, as they entered the design office, all such thoughts abruptly left her. Because it was in that office that she saw someone that she did know from Pillingers!

'Good morning,' Chris Nickson said generally to the two men and a woman at work there, as they went through to the chief designer's office.

There was a general response from two of them and Elyn offered her own 'good morning', but Hugh Burrell, still bearing a grudge, she noted from the cynical, un-smiling, sly-eyed way he looked at her, said not a word.

Elyn made a mental note to give the design section a wide berth, and subsequently finished her first month at Zappelli Fine China with that small incident the only thing that was in any way unpleasant.

Chris Nickson had asked her out a couple of times, and she liked him, but, since any date with him meant him calling for her, she wasn't too happy about intro-ducing him to her family, when any one of them was bound to say something derogatory about the firm he worked for.

She went to work on the first of February, outwardly looking as smart as paint, but feeling inwardly more than a little bit frazzled. Loraine had fallen for yet another of the Don Juan types that drew her like a magnet, and had again come out of the relationship licking her wounds.

'It's just not fair!' she had sobbed, and Elyn had been up with her half the night trying to get her to calm down.

Which, while Elyn was as keen as ever to get her teeth into some really absorbing work, made her not at all keen to meet any of that philandering type.

Not that she 'met' the owner of Zappelli Fine China exactly. It was more that she bumped into him. He was coming out of one door as she was going in and, bang, she came up against something solid. She rocked, but before she could lose her balance, in an instant a pair of strong firm hands were there on her arms to secure her.

Feeling slightly shaken, Elyn stepped back and, although fairly tall herself, looked up, and found herself looking straight into the cool, all-assessing dark-eyed gaze of a man she would know anywhere!

His photograph didn't do him justice, she observed at once as she took in Maximilian Zappelli's olive skin with a hint of bronze, his strong dark-as-night hair and aristocratic features. She made to go round him, and he let go of her—but not before he'd done a quick appraisal of her own fine features.

My stars! she fumed as his glance swept over her long honey-blonde hair, flawless complexion, and on to her suit with its expensive label. The man was a woman-eater!

'Excuse me, *signorina*,' he murmured, his apology for nearly knocking her off her feet sounding deliberately seductive, she thought, and as her insides, for the first time ever, did a quite idiotic somersault, she counteracted that she was in any way affected by the womaniser, and politely, if a touch arrogantly, she tilted her head a fraction and stepped past him.

She was first in at her department, and she was glad about that, because—and it was so ridiculous she could hardly believe it—she was shaking from the encounter. Without any trouble she recalled those dark liquid seductive eyes, recalled his barely accented English in those two words 'excuse me', and suddenly she was glad of her mother's experience. Glad of the experiences of her stepsister. Because, had she not known that there were such men around, she would have felt quite vulnerable. And she wasn't vulnerable, she knew she wasn't.

She got some work out of her desk drawer, but felt strangely on edge—so much so that she found she was hoping that this was just a fleeting visit by Signor Zappelli to his Pinwich factory. She wasn't afraid of him, of course, she scoffed. But somehow she felt she would rather not see him again.

CHAPTER TWO

By THAT afternoon, while having not forgotten the incident, Elyn was back on an even keel and was busily employed sifting through some averages when she realised she was some figures short. She glanced up to see that both Diana and Neil were absorbed in what they were doing, and left her chair.

'Design section,' she stated pleasantly, by way of letting them know where she would be if needed. She passed the tea dispenser on the way, however, and, noting Vivian and Ian, two members of the design staff, standing in a small queue, she almost did an about-turn. Hugh Burrell would probably be in the design section's outer office alone!

But—don't be ridiculous, her head took over from her feeling of wanting to return to her own office and avoiding anything unpleasant. She was more professional than that, wasn't she? In any case, it wasn't Hugh Burrell she wanted to see, but Brian Cole, his head of department.

She reached the design section door to recall how she had been more emotionally motivated than professional first thing that morning. Vowing to be more coolly professional when next she saw Maximilian Zappelli—and with luck this would be only a brief visit he was making to his English subsidiary—Elyn opened the door and went in.

Hugh Burrell *was* there. She gave him a courteous half-smile, which was received with a peevish look of ill-will. But since there was nothing she could do, or wanted to do, for that matter, to ease his personality problems, she carried on through to the chief designer's office.

That Brian Cole was not there was niggling on two counts: one that she would be held up for her figures, the other that Hugh Burrell could have told her his boss was out. Spotting a load of paperwork on Brian's desk, however, Elyn grew hopeful that he had left the figures she needed out for her.

Putting Hugh Burrell's rancorous attitude out of her mind, she sifted through the various pieces of paper at the side of his desk for anything that looked like what she was seeking. But some minutes later, she was still looking.

Realising that since her figure-work was not what Brian was most interested in and that there was every possibility that he hadn't found time yet to work out the breakdown she wanted, Elyn decided to find a scrap of paper and jot down a gentle reminder. Seeing how there was little free space on his huge desk, though, she decided against it.

Fortunately, Hugh Burrell had gone—probably to the tea machine—so she was spared another of his ill-natured looks, though she didn't see him as she returned to her own office. She was unable to complete her averages without that paperwork, though, so she found another small job to do for ten minutes.

That particular job completed, however, she was in the act of reaching for the internal phone in the hope that Brian was back, when suddenly the phone rang. 'Hello?' she said—and promptly got the shock of her life!

'Miss Talbot?' enquired a voice she would know anywhere.

So much for her hoping that this visit to his Pinwich subsidiary would be only fleeting—he was still here! 'Yes,' she answered, and heard what must be a natural trace of seduction in his voice, for it was there even when, authoritatively, he was issuing his orders.

And it was an order, there was no mistaking that, when 'Please to present yourself to Mr Cole's office immediately!' he commanded.

Left staring at the phone in her hand as his went down, Elyn felt her insides turn over again. This time, though, she'd had advance warning and wasn't bumping into him accidentally. This time, although she was mystified as to why, when she knew Maximilian Zappelli had an office in the building, she was being summoned to the design section—or summoned anywhere at all—she was going to be exceedingly professional.

Coolly professional, she reiterated, as she walked along the corridors. Coolly professional and pleasant, she decided, and entered the design office, to find it empty, but with the door to Brian Cole's office standing ajar.

She went over to it and, as before that day, was met in a doorway by Maximilian Zappelli. This time, though, they did not collide, because he stood back. 'Elyn Talbot?' he enquired, not by so much of a flicker of an eyelid revealing if he recalled their earlier meeting. 'Max Zappelli,' he introduced himself, stretching out a hand.

'How do you do,' she murmured, shaking his hand, but was more mystified than ever over what this was all about when, following him into Brian Cole's office, she saw that not only was Brian there, but his staff of three as well.

'I wonder if you can throw some light on a very serious matter that has come to our attention,' the head of Zappelli Fine China lost no time in coming to the point; as perfectly at home in her language as his own, Elyn noted.

'I will if I can,' she answered pleasantly. 'What...'

'Brian here has been working for some weeks now on a particularly fine sculpture involving a mix of bronze and ceramic. It is a design of the most intricate and beautiful. A design which, while still on paper, he is certain will work, but, because it breaks new ground, is of such uniqueness that any one of our competitors would give a lot to be first with.'

'How super!' she smiled, but was still mystified as to where she came into it. Quite clearly any mathematical calculations required on the design had been done without her help, or Brian Cole would not have been so certain that it would work. She was still feeling happy inside for Brian, though. 'But there's a problem?' she took a calculated guess.

'A very serious problem, Miss Talbot,' Maximilian Zappelli replied, giving her a level-eyed look. 'Some time today, between the hours of three and four, someone came into this office...' his eyes did not merely look into hers but seemed to pierce hers as if he could see into her very soul '... and removed the design from this desk.'

'No!' she gasped in astonishment, as 'removed' translated in her head to 'stole'. 'But I was in here myself at...' Her voice trailed off, and she looked wildly from him to the four others in the room, who she realised for the first time were looking at her—could it be—accusingly? Horrified, she swung her gaze back to the owner of the factory.

His stern gaze met hers full on, and she felt unable to look away. 'You were in here at a quarter to four,' he documented.

'Yes—yes, I was,' she answered in a rush—Hugh Burrell would have given him that information. 'I was short of some figures I wanted from Brian, so I came and...'

'But I did those figures! I took them to your office myself at lunchtime,' Vivian interrupted.

'So there was no need for you to be in here at all,' Hugh Burrell had to put in. 'You'd gone when I came back from Stationery, but there was no need for you...'

'Who did you give those figures to, Vivian?' Maximilian Zappelli chopped him off to ask.

'I didn't. They were all at lunch in the statistics department, so I left them by a computer, and...' Vivian's voice tailed off, and she looked apologetically at Elyn. Clearly, Elyn realised, in this computer age, Vivian thought everyone in the statistics section stayed glued to the computers all day long, and would return to the machines after lunch.

'You didn't see them?' the Italian asked Elyn coolly.

'No. I'd have had no need to have come looking for them if I had,' she defended, not meaning to be rude, but not at all liking the situation she was in.

'But you did come in here?'

'Yes. I saw Vivian and Ian at the tea dispenser...' She hesitated, and broke off, realising that she was feeling so unnerved that she seemed to be being accused that she was rattling on, and had been about to blurt out that she'd guessed Hugh Burrell would be there—and had almost turned back. Oh, how she wished she had! 'Anyhow...'

'You knew Brian was working on an outstanding design, and thought these offices would be empty?' the man she had dubbed philanderer swiftly misread her hesitation.

'No, I didn't!' she denied, a shade hotly, she had to own, with no sign of the cool professional she had determined to be as she faced her employer.

'According to this man here,' he ignored her show of spirit as he referred to Hugh Burrell, 'you were in this office alone for quite some time before he left.'

'I'd hoped to find Brian here,' she defended herself, starting to feel sick inside at the way this was going. 'I wanted those figures,' she stated, starting to feel a little desperate. 'I thought he might have left them on his desk for me.'

'You searched his desk?' he asked sharply.

'I *needed* those figures,' she reiterated.

'Was the design on the desk then?' he insisted, his tone sharp still, and Elyn started to feel even more desperate.

'I don't know! I wasn't looking for designs. I'm not interested in designs!' she exclaimed, her voice rising, even though she knew she was doing herself no good by not staying calm. But then she had never ever been accused of stealing anything in her life, or been so much as suspected of it, and she was not liking it very much, to say the least. 'Grief—why would I want any design—what would I do with it?' she asked—and suddenly went from agitated to staggered, when Hugh Burrell chose that moment to put the boot in.

'You'd know better than anyone what to do with it!' he tossed in spitefully—and all eyes turned to him.

Though it was the tall Italian who took him up on his comment. 'Would you care to explain that?' he suggested evenly—and it was clear to Elyn that Hugh Burrell could barely wait.

'I thought everybody knew,' he almost fell over himself to explain. 'Elyn Talbot's stepfather is Mr Samuel Pillinger of the now dead Pillinger Ceramics firm.' Elyn saw the start of surprise on the faces of the other members of the design team. Clearly, anyone who had known her from Pillingers had had much more interesting things to gossip about when she'd joined Zappelli's. She transferred her look back to Maximilian Zappelli, but could read nothing from his stern, masked expression. 'Her stepfather might have owned Pillingers,' Hugh Burrell went on to inform his listeners with relish, 'but until it went bust, it was Elyn Talbot who ran it. She'd know better than anyone who'd be dead keen to get hold of a design like that one!'

Well, that's it, Elyn thought. And, having just been neatly buried by Hugh Burrell, it was with a sinking heart that she realised how, from the evidence he had, and from what he had just heard, Maximilian Zappelli could only conclude that she was the one who had stolen the important design.

But, even as she tilted her chin defiantly and prepared to protest to the bitter end that she was not the guilty party, she saw his glance go from her to Hugh Burrell. His cool steady stare was back on her again, though, but when she was fully expecting him to go straight for her jugular, to her absolute astonishment, Maximilian Zappelli commented quietly, 'Thank you, Miss Talbot. I've no need to detain you further.'

Elyn stared back in disbelief. Though before she could utter a word, a strangled sort of cry caused her to switch her gaze from him to Hugh Burrell. He, she saw, was looking as totally amazed as she felt that it appeared their employer was saying—not that she was out, but that she was free to return to her office!

Quickly she pulled herself together to realise that she had nothing to thank any of them for. She took her eyes from Hugh Burrell and, inclining her head slightly in the direction of Maximilian Zappelli, she walked stiff-backed from the room. Somehow, though, she knew that was not the end of the matter.

Nor was it. She was not totally surprised, therefore, when at a few minutes before five that evening the internal phone rang.

'Hello,' she answered.

'Would you come to my office, please,' instructed a voice, then the phone went dead.

Elyn replaced her receiver. He had not asked who she was, and she'd had no need to ask who he was. Her guess was that she was about to be dismissed, and as she put her work away, she started to get angry. He might have done it on his own time, not hers! she fumed. It was always a rush to catch her train on time, and now she would miss it.

She was just debating whether, since she would be leaving soon—permanently—she'd catch her train anyway and leave Maximilian Zappelli waiting when, for some unknown reason, she suddenly felt compelled to go and see him.

'Night, Elyn,' Diana and Neil chorused as they left the office.

'Night,' she replied. 'See you tomorrow!' Fat chance, she knew, but somehow just that small act of friendly communication with the other two seemed to have cooled her anger.

Not that she wouldn't stick up for herself, she determined as she went in the general direction of Max Zappelli's office. Perhaps that was why she felt so compelled to go and see him—so he should know that she had not just guiltily slunk away. She promptly ceased all such musings when she came to what she was fairly certain was the door to his office.

'Come in,' invited a very faintly accented voice in answer to her knock.

Elyn defiantly squared her shoulders and entered a large room which had obviously been designed to create a relaxed atmosphere. A room perhaps where visiting business people were put at ease, she mused. For as well as a highly polished desk and a couple of upright chairs, there were also a couple of soothing-looking easy-chairs, and a matching soothing-looking settee.

She went further into the room, not knowing what to expect—perhaps a couple of security guards to escort her off the premises, or maybe, since that design was so valuable, even the police. But her employer was the only occupant. He was standing away from the desk, and somehow, as she looked up into his good-looking face, her insides churned, and a good deal of her defiance evaporated.

'You wanted to see me?' she enquired civilly, aware of his dark eyes assessing her, taking in her expensive suit.

'Please be seated,' he suggested, indicating a nearby chair.

By Elyn's reckoning, since she would soon be on her way out again, there seemed to be little point. But, since it seemed her dismissal was about to be served with some degree of politeness, she brought out her own good manners, and did as he suggested.

He did not sit down, though, but took a few steps away from her before suddenly turning round abruptly and, with a hand on his firm chin, his other hand thrust into the trouser pocket of his immaculately cut suit, demanded, 'Why did you hesitate when saying how you saw the two junior designers at the tea dispenser?' and Elyn blinked.

She blinked on two counts. One, that, having already challenged her that she had seen Vivian and Ian at the tea dispenser and had thought the design office would be empty, he was still pursuing that line of questioning,—the other that, by the look of it, her Italian employer was not going to dismiss her until he had everything he wanted to know.

'Well, Miss Talbot?' he insisted when it appeared she was too slow in answering.

His suddenly sharp tone annoyed her. 'Well,' she began, starting to actively dislike the man, 'I was on my way to the design section when I saw Vivian and Ian— which meant that Hugh Burrell might be in the outer office.'

'You didn't want to be alone with him?' Maximilian Zappelli concluded straight away. 'This man—he frightens you?'

'No!' she denied, wanting to leave it there—but soon realised that this issue was far too important, and that her employer was bent on extracting every bit of information in order to get at the truth—the truth, she saw, of her guilt.

'Why, then?' he demanded, and persisted. 'You shied at the thought of being alone with him?'

'Yes,' she had no alternative but to reply.

'He makes you feel uncomfortable?'

'I...' She broke off, but Max Zappelli had come that bit closer, and now, his hands at the sides of his desk as he leaned back and faced her and waited to be answered, she felt compelled to go on. 'I don't think it's so much that he makes me feel uncomfortable, but that I—well, that I just wanted to avoid any—unpleasantness.'

'Why would he be unpleasant to you?' he asked sharply before she could draw another breath.

'Because...' She broke off and threw him an exasperated look. 'Does it matter?' she asked shortly, her exasperation evident in her voice.

'You're suggesting that, because *you* find my questioning embarrassing, *I* should forget that the most important design ever produced at this factory has been stolen?' he demanded with arctic sarcasm. 'That because my questions displease you, I should not make any further attempt to get to the root of who stole it?'

'No, I'm n...' She broke off, her beautiful green eyes widening. 'Are you suggesting that you don't think I took it?' she dared to ask, realising from what he had just said that he could still be uncertain who had stolen the design, and might be prepared to consider that it hadn't been her.

For ageless moments Max Zappelli stared down into her wide-eyed look, then said toughly, 'I'm stating that I'm not blind, and that it was obvious to me in Brian Cole's office that Hugh Burrell, for some reason which I wish to eliminate before I go further, harbours feelings of malice against you.'

'Oh!' Elyn murmured, and was staggered at the sudden suspicion that the reason why he had aborted his questioning of her in the design chief's office was that he

had been perceptive enough to realise that Hugh Burrell
had been inwardly gloating as he'd revealed what he had
about her.

'*Now*,' Max Zappelli stressed, 'tell me why.'

'He—er—didn't take it very well when Pillingers had
to close down,' she admitted.

'I shouldn't think many of your employees were too
ecstatic!' the Italian commented drily, but was not to be
fobbed off. 'So, what else?'

Elyn sighed, wondering briefly, since she was still likely
to be dismissed anyway, if she needed this! Against that,
though, she didn't want any suspicion clinging to her
name. So, if this was what she had to do to attempt to
clear herself, so be it.

'So, he asked me out once, and I said no,' she told
him.

'You did not—um—fancy—him?'

'To be honest, no. But . . .'

'But?'

'Well, it's hardly relevant now, but I once dated
someone in the firm, and he seemed to think that to go
out with me meant he could expect special privileges at
work.' She shrugged. 'Come in late and leave early
without anyone saying anything—that sort of thing. I
made a rule after that not to date anyone from the
studios.'

For the first time Maximilian Zappelli nodded in
agreement. 'I have the same rule,' he commented, and
while Elyn, who had never lost sight of the 'philanderer'
label she had pinned on him, was doubting that any of
the elegant women she had seen him pictured squiring
around had ever done a hard day's nine-to-five graft
anyway, he was questioning, 'So you told him "no",
and he didn't like it, and seems to have waited for an
opportunity like today when, by revealing what you had
conveniently forgotten to put on your application form,
he could cause you maximum embarrassment.'

'It—er—wasn't quite like that,' she mumbled, realising that her interrogater must have given Chris
Nickson in Personnel a very thorough third degree about
her before he'd sent for her.

'No?' he questioned coolly.

'No,' she replied stiffly. 'Apart from nobody asking
me on the application if I was related to anyone who
ran a ceramic works——' Oh, grief, she thought when
she received a slight narrowing of his eyes for her trouble,
that hadn't gone down very well. 'I'm sorry,' she apologised, honestly accepting that she was in the wrong, 'I
know this isn't the time to be—flippant, but I'm a bit
on edge,' she understated. 'Anyhow,' she went on swiftly,
part of her wondering just what she'd apologised for, 'I
fully meant to tell Chris Nickson about my connection
with Pillingers, but—well, the moment just sort of got
away from me. I wanted the job, quite desperately *needed*
it,' she admitted, and could promptly have bitten her
tongue out as she realised that she had as good as told
him about her unsound finances. Dimwit, she scolded
herself. The last impression she wanted to give this astute
man was that she was so hard up that she'd resort to
dishonesty—to the extent of stealing a design—in order
to rectify the problem. 'And yes,' she sped on, 'I *was*
concerned that it might go against me if I said who I
was. Against that, though,' she hurried on, 'it seemed
to me that since there are a few ex-Pillinger people
working here, it would soon be out that Samuel
Pillinger's stepdaughter was working here.'

Having come to a rather rushed end, Elyn watch as,
without comment, Max Zappelli straightenéd away from
the desk and walked round to the other side of it. He
looked down at his desk, his face hidden, and she would
dearly have liked to know what he was thinking.

Then, with an abruptness she was learning to know,
he suddenly raised his head, and, while still standing,
looked straight at her with those soul-piercing dark eyes

and fired, 'You didn't think you might be dismissed when you were found out?'

She swallowed. Lord, he looked tough! 'Am I going to be?' she managed to enquire.

'For "omitting" to disclose your connections with a rival firm?'

She shook her head. 'That rival firm has ceased trading. I meant, am I going to be dismissed for that design of Brian Cole's that has gone missing.'

For a second or two those assessing dark eyes held her unflinching, if slightly apprehensive, green eyes. 'I hope I'm fairer than that,' he stated bluntly. 'When I find out for certain who took it I'll then set about dismissing the culprit.' Though before she could breathe a sigh of relief at that, he added, 'In the meantime, Miss Talbot, I want you where I can see you.'

From that, she gathered, she was still number one suspect. But, by the sound of it, she'd still got her job. She needed that job, but more important, she needed the money it paid. She stood up, words burning on her tongue to tell him what he could do with his job. But as it dawned on her that if word got out that she'd left Zappelli's with the suspicion that she was a thief still hanging over her, she would find it hopeless to get a job that paid even half as much as this one, she had to gulp down on her pride. 'Thank you,' was what she did say, and, with as much dignity as she could find, she left his office without another glance at him.

Elyn was still nursing bruised feelings the following Tuesday, a week later. So far as she knew—and she was going nowhere near the design section to find out—they hadn't discovered the person who'd stolen that design. Though so much for Max Zappelli's pronouncement of 'I want you where I can see you'—the latest word on the grapevine was that he'd returned to Italy the very next day!

Not that she wanted to see him, for goodness' sake. She could think of a dozen or so better occupations. But she was feeling restless, she had to own, though that was fully understandable, because until that culprit was found she was still under threat of dismissal—and that didn't stop the bills coming in.

The internal phone on her desk rang. Strangely, just lately, every time it rang, which luckily wasn't often, her heart would jump into her mouth. And you couldn't get stranger than that, she realised, as she said, 'Hello,' down the phone, because *he* was still in Italy and, so the grapevine had it, was not due to make another visit for a month at least.

'Hello Elyn, it's Chris,' the pleasant voice at the other end informed her, and instantly she was swamped by guilt. She had thought about contacting him to apologise because he might have heard a few short sharp comments from their employer to the effect that he should have found out about the Talbot-Pillinger connection before recommending her for employment. But she had delayed getting in touch with him, and when several days had elapsed without him contacting her either, she had assumed that perhaps he preferred not to have anything more to do with her.

But she answered warmly, 'Hello, Chris.' She liked him, and didn't want to be bad friends—then she realised he'd found her warm tone encouraging.

'I was wondering how you felt about going out with me tonight,' he told her without preliminaries.

'I... I think I should like to,' she smiled down the phone. She didn't want to go into details while they were both at work—and since he now knew of her family background, perhaps she could explain away any hostility they might show towards Zappelli's when he called for her, and also explain how nervous she had been that she might not get the job.

'Good,' he said, a sunny smile in his voice. 'I'll book a table somewhere—shall I call for you about seven?'

'That'll be fine,' she smiled, and realising he'd get her address from her application form, she added, 'Till then,' and put down the phone.

The internal phone did not ring again until ten past three that afternoon. This time, though, Elyn didn't get the chance to say 'Hello,' for, clearly impatient to be getting on, a very faintly accented voice demanded in a hurry, 'Miss Talbot?'

'Sp-speaking,' she answered, her heart racing—it was him! Was this it—her dismissal?

'Please to come and see me, *now*!' he ordered, and his line went dead.

Elyn put the phone down, stared at it, then spent the next two minutes in trying to calm herself. But three minutes later she was on her way to see Maximilian Zappelli, totally unaware that for the first time ever, she had not told Diana and Neil where she could be found.

By the time she had reached his office door, however, her brain patterns had sufficiently sorted themselves out for her to realise that if Max Zappelli was going to be true to his word, then it couldn't be that he had sent for her purely to dismiss her. She had not stolen that missing design, and he had most definitely said, 'I'll find out who took it—then set about dismissing the culprit'.

Even though she knew for certain that she was *not* the culprit, it was with a feeling of quite some trepidation, nevertheless, that Elyn knocked on his door. A moment later she was answering his 'Come in', and a moment after that she was once more in the company of the tall, sophisticated business-suited Italian.

'Good afternoon,' she greeted him formally—and found her greeting ignored as his glance flicked over her and another of her good quality suits.

'Take a seat, Miss Talbot,' he invited, much as he had before. This time, though, he waited no longer than to observe that she had taken a chair near his desk, before going round to the other side and taking a seat facing her.

His expression was bland, and she could tell little of what might be going on behind that clever forehead. But suddenly, since he was not being short and sharp with her, she began to wonder—had he sent for her in order to apologise? A flurry of excitement surged through her veins, and she guessed then that apologies didn't come easily to him.

Somehow then, ridiculously, she felt she wanted to help him out. 'Have you discovered who stole that valuable design?' blurted from her in an eager rush—but then she realised how idiotic she was being to imagine he would need her help in any way when his only answer was to study her eager expression for some long seconds.

Even so, she was still of the opinion that the thief must have been traced. Then at last, after what seemed like an age, her employer clipped, 'Unfortunately not!' and she straightaway realised she must still be the number one suspect, and every scrap of excitement and eagerness faded.

'I suppose it will do no good for me to insist that I didn't take it?' she suggested flatly.

'You have other skills, I believe,' he responded evenly, and Elyn, feelings of hostility against him beginning to stir, stared back woodenly at him.

'Other than thievery, you mean?'

He ignored her sarcasm, not a scrap dented by it, surveying her with a cool arrogant look. 'Tell me about your training, Miss Talbot,' he commanded.

'Training?' She felt somewhat confused, feeling sure he was within an ace of telling her to leave and not come back, yet feeling too as if he was about to do the sort of in-depth interview which maybe he believed someone should have done at the outset. Even if, in her opinion, she considered her interview had been quite thorough.

'Training—qualifications,' he drawled in enlightenment, and suddenly Elyn's feelings towards him were most definitely hostile. He knew, simply knew, since without question he'd personally scrutinised everything Personnel held on her, that her qualifications were so limited they were next door to being non-existent!

Unconsciously, as she decided to ignore his question about qualifications, Elyn tilted her chin an arrogant warring degree or two. 'I have had the soundest training,' she stated coolly, looking unflinchingly into the dark fathomless eyes that calmly surveyed her. 'I left school at sixteen,' she confirmed the entry on her application form, and went on to reveal something which was not. 'I then spent six months working in each of the various departments at my stepfather's firm, before gravitating to the administration side of the business—where I at once realised I felt happiest.'

'You're comfortable with figures and administration?' Max Zappelli slotted in, his dark gaze steady on her face.

'Yes, I am,' she agreed, seeing no sense in denying the truth of that.

'According to Hugh Burrell, you ran Pillingers.'

Was Max Zappelli trying to trip her up? 'I wouldn't say that exactly,' she answered. 'Naturally I referred to my stepfather on anything I couldn't handle.'

'But most of the time you acted on your own?' he suggested.

Elyn had a hard time hiding the exasperation she felt with this man. But, since it didn't appear that he had it in mind to dismiss her, and since she needed the income from this job, she swallowed hard on her feelings, to reply honestly, 'The office side of things was smooth-running; there was little I had to do but attend to the day-to-day affairs.'

'You were that good?'

Elyn looked at him in some perplexity. What the dickens was he getting at? Coolly, though, he eyed her back, just waiting. She smothered a flicker of annoyance, and again reminded herself that he was the one who paid her wages. 'If by "good" you mean that the place ran with barely a hiccup, then yes,' she asserted herself to throw away modestly, 'yes, I was that good.'

Hardly were the words out of her mouth, though, when she knew from the sudden aggressive look that came to his eyes that perhaps modesty might have been the better part of valour. Nor was she mistaken about that aggression, she realised. 'So good, in fact,' Max Zappelli took up toughly, 'that when you should have seen Pillinger's crash coming ten kilometres away, you did not!' Elyn's astonishment at his words was so great, she just sat and stared at him open-mouthed. But her astonishment went from mere astonishment to utter incredulity as he went on, 'I'm afraid, Miss Talbot, that you have a lot to learn!' And while she was still staring indignantly at him, he pronounced, 'Which is why I have decided to send you to Italy for further training.'

'*Italy*!' she exclaimed, absolutely thunderstruck.

'That is what I said,' he replied curtly, and there was something in his tone which brooked no argument, when he sharply declared 'I think we'll have you in Italy without any further delay!'

CHAPTER THREE

THERE might have been a note in Max Zappelli's voice that there was no arguing with, but that didn't stop Elyn from trying. 'Italy!' she gasped again.

But suddenly his tone had changed, and there was a mocking light in his eyes. 'It *is* on this planet,' he drawled. 'Less than two hours' flying time away, in fact.'

'Yes, but ...' she was still reeling and floundering because of it '...but what training do I need?' she asked— and why Italy, for goodness' sake? 'So far as I know— and I'm sure I'm right,' she inserted hurriedly, 'the statistics section is running on oiled wheels.'

'Computers!' he threw at her with a rapidity that made her blink. 'How up to date is your training on computers?'

Elyn bit her lip—a dead giveaway, she realised too late, that the computers she'd worked on at Pillingers had been a little outdated. It was true, too, that since working at Zappelli's she had thrown her concentration more into setting up the section and getting it going than taking time out to master machinery new to her. Swiftly, though, she tried to make her expression untroubled as, reasonably she thought, she pointed out, 'I can't be expected to be up to date on *all* computers. New technology is coming in all the time,' she began to warm to her theme, only to be promptly floored when Max Zappelli chipped in to agree with her.

'Exactly,' he stated, with the hint of a clever smile on his face—which she didn't trust one iota, and knew she was right not to trust when he added, 'I think you will

find that our Verona offices have the most recent tech-
nological equipment.'

'Ver...' She broke off as she tried desperately to as-
semble an argument. 'But why Verona? I'm sure there
must be dozens of computer training establishments in
England without my having to...'

'You have some special reason for not wanting to leave
England?' he cut in sharply. 'Some man friend, perhaps,
some lover!' he rapped.

For a man who was never without some lovely on his
arm, he'd got some nerve! Elyn fumed. But, oddly, it
seemed a point of honour that he didn't know there
weren't too many exciting men around in the Pinwich
and Bovington areas, so she retorted, 'Naturally, I've
got men friends.'

'But no one in particular,' he said as quick as a flash.

'I'm working on it!'

'You can continue to work out your strategy while
you're in Italy,' he bounced at her, and Elyn gave him
a speaking look. But, as she was still determined not to
go, still determined to find some way of getting out of
going, she realised that the shrewd Italian must have read
her determination in her look. He certainly played his
ace card at any rate when, clearly not having forgotten
how last Tuesday she had said she wanted and desperately needed this job, he quietly let fall, 'Naturally your
stay in Verona will be expenses-paid, and your whole
salary will continue to be paid into your bank.'

Swine! she fumed, but knew she hadn't got a leg to
stand on. She needed that salary, and he was calling the
shots. But then, hearing him talk of her salary being
paid into her bank, she began to wonder how long this
'training session' would take.

'How long would I be away?' she ventured, while still
mentally fighting against going.

Coolly his gaze swept her unsmiling face, then, almost
as if he was enjoying himself hugely, he dropped out

blandly, 'You'll find you'll have good instructors—I'm sure they'll have you totally computer-friendly by Easter.'

Easter! She'd been thinking in terms of days, not weeks! 'When would I have to go?' she asked, her mind alive with excuses for being unable to travel at the last moment.

His answer was to glance at his watch. 'I'm returning to Verona myself early this evening—there will be room on the plane for you if...'

'I can't be ready by then!' she exclaimed. This was all happening too fast! She liked to be the one in charge of her own destiny, but this man was sweeping her along like a tidal wave. 'Even if I left the office now, this minute, I'd never...'

'Point taken,' he cut in, but before she could take heart that he was taking the pressure off, he was putting the pressure on again by telling her, 'Make it tomorrow.' She opened her mouth to protest, but he beat her to it. 'You'd better go home now, come to think of it—you've a lot to do.'

Magnanimous yet! She'd have her work cut out getting ready to fly out tomorrow for goodness knew how long. 'Oh!' she exclaimed suddenly, as she remembered something.

'Problem?' he queried.

'I'm supposed to have a date tonight.'

His answer was to push the phone towards her. 'Feel free,' he invited.

Elyn shook her head. It wasn't the outside phone that she wanted. 'I'll cancel it later,' she said, and when her employer actually smiled, revealing perfect teeth as his generous mouth curved upwards, Elyn knew that his smile wasn't because he had caused her to cancel her date, but because in her statement that she would cancel it lay her acceptance that at some time tomorrow she would be on a flight to Verona. 'I can't speak Italian,' was the only protest she had left to make.

Maximilian Zappelli stood up, tall and powerful in business and physique. 'Five and five add up to ten in any language,' he told her succinctly. The interview was over.

An hour later Elyn was on the train on her way home, her head full of things she should have asked but hadn't. Things she should know but didn't. And with a feeling that, when most people would give anything for the chance to go to Italy for some training, she was kicking like crazy against it. When she tried to analyse quite why she objected, she could find no answer. All she knew was that she had an instinctive gut reaction against going.

Was it perhaps, she wondered, because she'd been *told* that she was to go, and not *asked*? Not that she could see Max Zappelli asking for anything—he demanded and got, and she didn't like it! Elyn sighed as she got out of the train at Bovington. All she hoped was that the Verona plant was large enough so that she would not be bumping into him every five minutes.

She set off on the walk to her home, recalling how Chris Nickson had taken it very well when she'd contacted him to say that she couldn't make their date that evening, and why.

'Lucky you!' he'd exclaimed, going on to state that he'd heard of some of their art people going over for a look round and that other office executives might well have gone over for training, but, as he was fairly new to the company himself, he hadn't any knowledge of it.

'As you said, Chris, lucky me,' Elyn responded, only then fully accepting that, because she couldn't get out of it, she would have to go.

'When will you be back?' asked Chris.

'I'm not sure,' she told him, and wished she knew the answer to that one herself, though she knew she was going to work hard, the sooner to return.

'You won't forget you owe me a date when you are back?'

'Not for a minute,' she smiled, and rang off.

Elyn let herself in through the front door of her home, aware that telling Chris Nickson where she was going was the easy part—now she had to break it to her family.

'You're home early!' her mother exclaimed, coming out into the hall.

'I've a lot to do,' Elyn began, and went with her mother into the drawing-room where, with the exception of Loraine, the rest of her family were.

To her surprise, though she was careful to leave out the name Zappelli, her mother and stepfather took it much better than she had supposed. Though not so her stepbrother.

'What in the blue blazes are you going for?' he questioned sulkily.

'I've just told you,' she said, and explained patiently, 'My computer skills aren't what they should be so...'

'So you're going deep into the enemy camp!' he cut her off angrily.

'Oh, don't be like that, Guy!' Elyn implored. 'I need this job, I...'

'No, you don't. You've still got some money left over from the sale of your car.'

It was true she had, but she also had an absolute dread of debt, and that remaining money, besides being put by for the next round of bills, was there too to allow for such unexpected expenditure as might crop up, such as slates off the roof.

Elyn didn't want to argue with Guy, though; he was as dear to her as if he were her own brother. 'I'd better go and start packing. I can do quite a lot before dinner,' she said.

'Don't forget to pack your snow-boots,' Guy prompted belligerently.

Elyn left them and went up to her room, to realise only then that at this time of year Verona could well be carpeted in thick snow. Guy hadn't meant to be helpful, she knew, but thanks to his comment, she decided she had better get her snow-boots out.

Her mind was as busy as her hands in the next hour as she began to pile things which she would ultimately load into a suitcase on to her bed. It was all very well for *him* to announce, 'I've decided to send you to Italy,' but it would have been a great help if he'd also announced by what plane, and where she was to stay when she got there!

After about an hour of sending hate vibes to where *he* might be, however, her sense of fairness—which she was beginning to dislike as much as she disliked him—began to assert itself. He *had* offered to give her a lift in his plane—no doubt a private executive jet. Not that she could have been ready so soon. And, if she was honest, then she had allowed him to keep the impression which Hugh Burrell had given him that she was head cook and bottlewasher at Pillingers. So Max Zappelli could hardly be blamed for thinking if she was that clever it wouldn't be beyond her capabilities to book a flight for herself for the next day, and for her to also arrange her own hotel accommodation.

The phone in her room rang just as she had the door open to go down to dinner, and, as no one else seemed inclined to take the call, Elyn went back to answer it.

'May I speak to Miss Elyn Talbot?' a female accented voice requested.

'Speaking,' said Elyn.

'Ah—my name is Felicita Rocca; I am the personal assistant to the Signor Zappelli,' she introduced herself.

'Oh, hello!' Elyn exclaimed in surprise.

'Hello,' Felicita answered, a smile in her voice, and getting down to the reason for her call, 'Signor Zappelli has given instructions for me to arrange your flight— have you a pen?' she enquired.

Five minutes later Elyn, suddenly feeling a whole lot better about her departure tomorrow, made her way down the stairs. 'What's the name of your hotel?' asked her mother as they sat down to the meal.

Elyn smiled. 'I don't know yet, but someone will be at Verona airport to meet me.'

She returned to her room to finish her packing, and wondered if it would be a company chauffeur who would be at the airport to meet her. Since her plane wasn't scheduled to land until late afternoon she doubted that Felicita Rocca would be there. Though since from her phone call tonight it was evident that she didn't always finish work on the stroke of five, it was a possibility, she supposed.

For some technical reason, however, her plane was late departing from London the following afternoon. Since there was nothing she could do about it, all Elyn could hope was that someone would ring to check the plane's time of arrival before they left to meet her.

It worried her for some while that someone would be kept hanging about waiting for her. But once into the flight, her thoughts started to become more and more centred on her employer. She did not want to think about him, but all at once she didn't seem able to get him out of her head. If she looked out of the window her thoughts were soon away from the darkening sky outside, and were on him. She concentrated on her meal, but only to discover that she was wondering—would he really bring her to Italy to brush up her skills if he truly believed she was a crook? Would he, in all seriousness, so much as consider bringing her to where he had his main work-place—the same place where he mainly worked—if he thought for a moment that she might be some kind of industrial spy?

Feeling impatient with herself, Elyn tidied up her meal tray and sat back in her seat. Oh, bother the man, she fumed, and concentrated firmly on how hard and fast the stewardesses worked—and found she was recalling how Max Zappelli had stated, quite categorically, that he wanted her where he could see her. And, as that un-palatable truth hit home, Elyn realised that, while it was true that her computer skills could do with an update, the main reason for her being brought to Verona to work was that Max Zappelli didn't want her far from his sight. Which in turn answered the question, would he allow her anywhere near his Verona establishment while be-lieving her a thief? Yes, came the answer, he jolly well would!

Which was just fine and dandy, Elyn fumed crossly, not liking at all the thought that she was still as much under suspicion as ever. Oh if only she could be inde-pendent and tell him what he could do with his job!

But she was not independent—she needed her job. Maybe her horror of unpaid bills stemmed from the hand-to-mouth existence she and her mother had had— even before her father had left for good. Perhaps mixed in there too was a feeling that since Sam Pillinger had put an end to all that scraping along when he had married her mother, she felt she owed him something. Whatever the reason, though, the thought of being insolvent was nightmarish to her. So, until such time as her family came to terms with the demise of Pillinger Ceramics, and ac-cepted that it might be an idea for a couple of them to find some paid employment, she would stick it out at Zappelli Fine China.

Any ensuing thought that, conversely, her employers could dispense with her services whenever they felt like it was promptly taken out of her head when having been circling over Verona airport for some time, apparently, the pilot announced that because of fog they were di-verting to another airport.

Oh lord, Elyn fretted, now what did she do? She was being met at Verona, and her plane was landing heaven knew where! The pilot had said, but she hadn't caught the name.

It was not too long afterwards, however, that the plane began to descend. Though by the time it had landed, Elyn realised, having put on her watch an hour to Italian time, that the offices of Zappelli Fine China in Verona would have closed some time ago.

Making contingency plans as she went, she made her way through Passport Control and Customs. She was on her way to the exit with her luggage, however, when it came to her to wonder if whoever had been delegated to meet her in Verona would have possibly put a call through with some message for her.

She stopped and put down her case and her flight bag, pulling them close into her so no one should trip over them. Then she turned and looked about for an information desk, or maybe some likely-looking official who could direct her.

Then suddenly, like music in her ears, a voice she would know anywhere, a voice that had, to her ears, a naturally seductive quality, said those magical words, 'Hello, Elyn.'

In an instant she spun round, a peculiar sensation of delight making itself felt within her, while a smile she could do nothing about, and which started somewhere at the tips of her toes, lit her face. 'Oh, hello,' she said huskily, and stood there smiling like an idiot while solemnly, silently, Max Zappelli's gaze roved her fine complexion, lovely green eyes and exquisite mouth.

Then, his gaze still on her beaming face, he stated quietly, 'You, Elyn Talbot, are very beautiful.'

'Oh!' she exclaimed. His compliment was so unexpected, she didn't know how to answer him.

'Your smile of relief that you are not stranded lights up your beauty,' he explained, and in the next instant he was hefting up her case and flight bag and instructing, 'Come—I am illegally parked.'

Somewhat startled, Elyn chased after his striding figure. He was quite dishy himself, but she'd cut out her tongue before she'd let him know that thought. She was sitting beside him in his Ferrari, her luggage stowed, when she accepted that she must have been more strung up than she'd realised at the possibility of being stranded. The last time she'd seen Max Zappelli—only yesterday, in fact—she'd felt more like burying an axe in his head than grinning at him like a demented idiot.

She watched as he expertly manoeuvred his car through the traffic, but it was some minutes later, as they stopped at a motorway tollgate, that she felt recovered enough to offer her thanks.

'I appreciate you coming to meet me,' she offered pleasantly, and as he turned to glance at her, she added politely, 'Thank you.'

He moved his eyes from her and started up his car again, and as they began to speed up the motorway, he explained, 'My home lies midway between Verona and Bergamo. I was on my way there when Felicita contacted me by car phone to say your flight had been switched to Bergamo airport.' He flicked a glance at her, but was still concentrating on his driving. 'I was almost halfway to Bergamo at that time,' he shrugged. 'I told her to recall the driver and that I would meet you myself.'

'Well, thank you again,' Elyn murmured. She hadn't expected him to be the one to meet her at the airport in Verona anyway, so she couldn't understand why she should feel miffed that he had never planned to meet her. 'I hope I haven't inconvenienced you too much,' she added, with more good manners than a hundred per cent sincerity. This man suspected her of being a thief, for goodness' sake—why should she thank him for anything?

'Not at all,' he replied suavely. 'My engagement this evening is not until much later.'

Philandering swine! she muttered to herself, and gave her attention to looking out of the window. So much for bringing her snow-boots—there wasn't a scrap of snow!

There was fog, though, and they hit it with a suddenness which Elyn wasn't ready for. Max Zappelli was, though, she observed, and, whatever her mutinous thoughts against him, she had to admire the way he swiftly reacted to reduce their speed.

She stayed quiet, however, and left him to give all his attention to getting them to Verona in one piece. Which, despite the fog, he managed to achieve in about an hour from the time they had left Bergamo.

'Er—where will I be staying?' she enquired as he seemed to be driving towards the outskirts and not towards any central hotel area.

'My apologies, Elyn,' he said at once, 'I should have told you,' and, rectifying that omission, 'We have a company apartment which we keep for visiting business people. I thought, or rather Felicita thought, that you would be happier there than in a hotel.'

'That's very kind of y... of Felicita,' Elyn responded. Really, for someone who had doubts about her honesty, he was being rather good, taking heed of his PA's comments like that. It was the second time he'd called her by her first name too. Perhaps he wasn't such a bad sort after all, she found herself thinking.

The company flat was in a smart area, with a front desk that was guarded by a stocky but well muscled man in his forties. '*Buona sera, signorina, buona sera, signore,*' he greeted them respectfully.

'*Buona sera,* Uberto,' Max Zappelli replied, and as Uberto immediately sprang into action and made as if to relieve him of her suitcase, her employer declined his offer, and in a flurry of what was to her totally incomprehensible Italian appeared to give him some instructions. Then, switching just as comfortably to English, 'Between them, Uberto, and Paolo during the day, will attend to your security here. There should be no problems with the apartment, but do not hesitate to contact either of them if you need assistance in any way.'

'Thank you,' she murmured politely, and with a friendly smile to Uberto in passing, she went with her employer to the lift and travelled up with him to the third floor. 'I can carry my flight bag,' she suggested belatedly as he hefted her case out of the lift.

Her suggestion was ignored, so she trailed after him until he reached a certain door in the hall, setting down her case, produced a key and unlocked the door, and held it open for her to precede him into what she quickly saw was quite a luxurious apartment.

The hall and sitting-room at any rate were covered in thick-pile palest green carpet, and the quite large sitting-room was well and elegantly furnished.

'You will be comfortable here?' Max Zappelli enquired, following her in, his eyes watching as her glance went from occasional tables to pictures on the walls and to a most comfortable-looking three-piece suite.

Her own home was elegant too. Her mother had excellent taste and, let loose with some money after her marriage to Sam, she had gradually changed some of the furniture and furnishings to those more to her own taste. 'Yes,' Elyn answered all the same, 'I'm sure I shall,' and decided to check out the other rooms in the apartment later.

He half turned as though to go, and oddly, she had the strangest impression that he somehow seemed reluctant to leave. Which was just plain ridiculous. She might, purely from the newness of it all, not be too eager to be left on her own, but he, for goodness' sake, must be keen to get away. He'd got a date fixed for later that evening, he'd as good as said so—and he'd got to go through the fog again and get home and change yet.

'Er—thank you once again for meeting me at the airport,' she said hurriedly, and knew, since some female was obviously waiting for him, that he considered he'd done all that he needed when, turning back to her, he passed the keys of the apartment to her. The touch of his hand send a *frisson* of electricity through her.

'Goodnight, Elyn,' he bade her quietly.

But she was still a little stunned from that unexpected tingle from the feel of his skin, and for the moment she could not find her tongue to offer him even the simplest of parting words. Had she been a little stunned before, however, she was quite enormously shaken when, leaning forward, he did no more than, albeit briefly, place a warm and yet more electrifying kiss on first one cheek and then the other—and suddenly Elyn was galvanised into action. Abruptly her hands came up and she pushed him away, while at the same time she took a hasty step backwards—and earned herself his amusement for her trouble.

Naturally, she fumed, he just couldn't accept without comment that there might be some women who weren't falling over themselves for his kisses. Neither did he, but, as he rocked back on his heels, there was mockery in his eyes. 'Relax, frigid little virgin,' he began. 'I...'

But Elyn was on edge, and swiftly, sharply—too swiftly, she afterwards realised—the words burst from her in a gasp of surprise. 'How did you know?'

'I...' He broke off, the mockery replaced by a look of incredulity. 'You're not?' he questioned.

Elyn rapidly pulled herself together, and took another step back from him, her head coming up haughtily as she retorted with cold arrogance, 'That's none of your business!'

Had she thought, though, that her uppity manner might result in him getting on his high horse and putting a swift end to this conversation, then she discovered that she couldn't have been more wrong. Because, as he started to look more incredulous than ever, he gave some short Italian exclamation and, unmoved by her arrogance, 'You are!' he reverted to English to state in wonder.

'If I am, I am!' she retorted, and before he could find a mocking answer to that, 'Thank you very much for meeting me at the airport,' she went on, and, talking straight on through the gentle-seeming smile that came over his face, 'but now, presuming you want me to be in the office for nine tomorrow, I'd like to set about unpacking.'

She saw him check his smile, but didn't like the mocking grin that replaced it any better as he drawled, 'I do believe you are throwing me out of my own property.'

'Goodnight, Mr Zappelli,' she said firmly, unsmiling.

'Oh, goodnight, Miss Talbot,' he grinned, 'goodnight,' and taking her none too gentle hint, he went.

Philandering swine! Elyn fumed, though she was caught by a pang of loneliness once the door had closed after him. Moving from the sitting-room into an equally splendid bedroom, she decided it was no wonder she should have felt a tiny bit lonely. After all, here she was, alone in Italy, a foreign land, when not too many hours ago she had been in England, in her home where there was always someone there to talk to.

She had got no further than hauling her suitcase on to the bed prior to starting to unpack it, though, before Max Zappelli was back in her thoughts again. Damn the man, he just wouldn't stay out! Diabolical philanderer, she dubbed him again: womanising came as second nature to him!

Against that, though, hadn't he told her himself that he never dated any of his staff? Not that he'd asked her for a date or anything like that. But to salute her on both cheeks the way he had—when they weren't even friends— was a shade disconcerting, she had to own.

When finally Elyn went to bed she confessed to being to some degree mixed up. She certainly had no time for philandering Romeos—yet here she was in Verona, literally the heart of Romeo territory. And when at one time she had been certain that she hated Max Zappelli, she was confused about that too. But, as she closed her eyes and willed sleep to come, she admitted that she was still left wondering—was he philandering or, in bestowing those electrifying kisses to her cheeks, was he merely being just a perfectly polite Italian?

CHAPTER FOUR

ELYN awoke on Thursday determined she would take nothing at face value where Signor Maximilian Zappelli was concerned. His kisses on her cheeks in parting last night might well have been a mere courtesy, but from now on she would treat the philanderer with the utmost caution.

She was in the middle of trying to dissect just why, when he thought her a thief, he should kiss her anyway, when she suddenly brought herself up short. Grief, she had far better things to do than to give him so much time in her head!

In the next moment Elyn was out of bed. A minute after that and she was getting ready to start her day. She was dressed and ready and on the point of going down to Uberto, or Paolo, if he should be the one on duty, to seek help and directions for getting to her new place of work, when she received a call from Uberto over the apartment's internal speaker system.

'Hello?' she offered.

'*Buon giorno, signorina*,' he said, and there followed a whole stream of Italian which she had no hope of understanding. Though, while she accepted that she could well be wrong, she thought she had picked out a couple of words that sounded just like 'Signorina Rocca'.

'*Grazie*,' she thanked him, using one of the very few Italian words she knew, and decided that since she had been going down to see Uberto anyway, she would go now and hopefully find out what the 'Signorina Rocca' had all been about.

She was happy to discover that she *had* picked up the name of Max Zappelli's PA correctly; for as she stepped out of the lift, a dark-haired and very attractive woman of about thirty, after a quick word with Uberto who had obviously told her who she was, came away from his desk stretching out a hand. '*Buon giorno*, Elyn,' she greeted her warmly, 'I'm Felicita,' and as they shook hands, 'You had a good flight?'

'Apart from the fog.'

'Ah, but today the fog is gone,' Felicita smiled, 'and we should be in our work on time.'

'How kind of you to think to call in to give me a lift to the office,' Elyn thanked her, as they walked out of the building to where Felicita had her Fiat parked.

The journey to Zappelli Internazionale did not take long, and Elyn again thought how kind Felicita was when, instead of leaving her at Reception for someone to come and claim her, she personally took her along to the section she would be working in. There were several people in the computer section, and Felicita introduced her around before coming to a halt by a bespectacled man of medium height who was in his early twenties. 'This is Tino Agosta, with whom you will be working. Tino,' she added, 'has excellent English.'

'How do you do,' smiled Elyn, and as Felicita departed, she began her first day at Zappelli Internazionale.

Tino, she soon learned, as well as speaking excellent English, was also something of a wizard on computers. It was eleven o'clock, though, when she was just getting the hang of something he was teaching her, that he suggested they break now for coffee.

'I was just getting into that!' she exclaimed.

'But I think we must now rest our eyes, Elyn,' he said solemnly, and Elyn argued no more, but went with him to the staff canteen, and, after a cup of the strongest coffee she had ever tasted, decided she would quench her thirst with something else tomorrow.

When lunchtime arrived Elyn realised that if she was to return the compliment and pay for Tino's tea that afternoon the way he'd paid for her coffee that morning, she had better get herself to a bank.

'Is there a bank near here,' she asked him.

'I shall come with you,' he answered.

'Oh, but your lunch?'

'I can eat later,' he shrugged, and Elyn started to really like him.

'I need to buy a few provisions—milk, bread,' she told him, and was grateful again to Tino when he went with her to help with her purchases. 'I'll be able to do this on my own next week,' she told him as they went back to Zappelli Internazionale and headed for the canteen for a quick something to eat.

The afternoon sped by, with Tino enquiring a little anxiously as they prepared to bed the machinery for the night, 'I hope the day has not been too boring for you?'

'I found it most absorbing,' Elyn assured him, and decided she thought Italian people were lovely when just then Felicita Rocca popped her head round the door and offered her a lift home. 'Do you have to pass the apartment to get to your own home?' Elyn asked her as they got into the Fiat.

'No, but it is no trouble to come for you,' Felicita answered her, but at that Elyn closely watched the route they took. Tomorrow she would make her own way to the office.

Felicita protested when she told her, but Elyn insisted. 'I like to walk,' she explained, 'and it will also give me a chance to get my bearings.'

'If you are sure?' Felicita questioned.

'I'm sure,' Elyn smiled, and thanking her, went inside the apartment building to see a man of similar age, shape and build to Uberto and similarly uniformed. '*Buona sera,* Paolo,' she smiled pleasantly as she went by to the lift.

She discovered he was as good at guessing correctly too, though her appalling Italian accent might have given away the fact that she was the new English resident, she realised when, favouring her with the widest grin imaginable, he beamed, '*Buona sera*, Signorina Talbot.'

Having been with people all day, Elyn had only been home an hour when she began to feel decidedly lonely. Don't be ridiculous! she told herself. It was only that everything was all so new. Once she got the feel of the place, she'd feel at home.

Of course, she wasn't going to be here all that long, she mused, and somehow, at that thought, she began to feel more unsettled than ever. Grief, she wasn't *that* lonely that she was going off her head, was she? She'd met some really super Italian people today, but there was one whom she wouldn't mind if she never saw again.

Not that she'd had much opportunity that day. If he'd been around, she certainly hadn't seen him. So—so much for her decision that she would treat Max Zappelli with the utmost caution in future—chance would be a fine thing!

At that thought, though, her innate honesty popped out for an alarming airing. And suddenly she was rocked to her foundations. Heavens above, she reeled, for a moment there it had seemed every bit as though she was *attracted* to the wretched man, and was *piqued* that she hadn't seen him! As if it wasn't loneliness that unsettled her, but that she was unsettled, *because* of him!

Ridiculous, said her head, totally ridiculous. Though when later Elyn went to bed, it was with the realisation that she had thought of little else but him all night.

By morning, however, she was once more back on an even keel. Drat the man, it was more that she found it upsetting that anyone should think her dishonest that kept him in her thoughts than anything else.

Elyn walked to work, and, to counteract any notion that she was in any way attracted to the head of Zappelli

Internazionale, when Tino Agosta shyly asked her to have dinner with him that night, after barely any hesitation, she agreed.

'I am delighted,' he smiled, and after a few minutes spent in discussing where they would eat, with Elyn giving him her address so he could call for her, they got down to some work.

It was a busy but pleasant morning, and at lunchtime Elyn went out to stretch her legs, and found herself in a busy shopping area. She was window-gazing at one of the city's high-class stores, though, when who should come by but Felicita Rocca. They walked back to the office together.

'You discovered your way this morning without problem?' Felicita enquired, and when Elyn replied that she had, 'You are enjoying your work with Tino?' she asked.

'Very much,' Elyn answered truthfully. 'Some of it is quite complex, but Tino is very patient.'

'He is a very clever young man,' Felicita stated what Elyn had already seen for herself, and they chatted on for a few minutes until Felicita asked her if she had any plans for the forthcoming weekend.

It was a matter of pride to Elyn that Felicita should not form an impression of her going back to the apartment that night to just sit there doing nothing but wait for Monday to roll around. She'd just die of embarrassment if the kindly woman should feel in any small way responsible for her.

'I've rather a full weekend planned, actually,' she answered, and, realising she just couldn't leave it at that, 'This is my first time in Italy, so I thought I'd get in as much sightseeing as I can on Saturday and Sunday. Though tonight Tino is taking me to his favourite restaurant for a meal.'

'Good,' smiled Felicita. 'You and Tino must be working well together,' she commented, and the re-

mainder of their walk back to Zappelli Internazionale
was taken up with Felicita telling Elyn of places of
interest which she might like to visit.

Elyn had been back at work for about an hour when
Tino broke off his instruction to answer the internal
telephone. She guessed, however, when his manner suddenly became totally alert and respectful, that he had
someone very important on the other end. But she was
surprised when replacing the telephone, Tino turned to
her and said, 'Signor Zappelli wishes to see you, Elyn.'

Her mouth fell open in a small 'O', but she murmured, 'Ah', and, 'Now?' she queried.

'I will show you the way,' he volunteered at once and,
rather than keep the head of Zappelli Internazionale
waiting, he was already on his feet.

Elyn was wearing a smart black skirt teamed with a
black and white check jacket, and, giving her jacket a
neatening tug, she went with Tino through a maze of
corridors and up a couple of flights of stairs.

'I will leave you here,' he told her, halting at one particular door. 'Will you be able to find your way back?'

'Yes, I'm sure,' she replied with more hope than
certainty.

Tino smiled. In her view, he was clearly of the opinion
that their employer, remembering she was a foreigner in
their midst, must want to have a personal welcoming
word with her. Then he went back the way he had come.

But, tapping politely on the door in front of her, Elyn
was more inclined to think that Max Zappelli, who still
had doubts about her honesty, was more likely to want
to say a personal and permanent farewell than to personally welcome her.

When, in response to her knock, an English 'Come
in!' reached her ears, she realised that he was supremely
confident that she would not keep him waiting.

And that annoyed her, made her wish she had
dawdled. If she was about to be dismissed then she

wished he'd done that in England rather than drag her all this way. In point of fact, she heartily wished she had resigned and taken the choice from him. When promptly on the heels of that thought, though, Elyn thought of how the day-to-day living expenses would be mounting up back home, rebellion left her. She turned the door handle—Max Zappelli might have a choice, but she most definitely did not.

'Ah, Elyn!' He stood up as she went in. 'Come and take a seat.' Elyn moved across to the seat at the other side of his desk, mentally wary about what all this was about. 'You've settled in comfortably, I hope?' he enquired pleasantly, and, as she sat down, he resumed his seat.

'Yes, thank you,' she replied with equal pleasantness. If he was dismissing her, he was going about it in the oddest way.

'You and Tino Agosta are—compatible?'

'Most compatible.'

'Would you mind, I wonder, saying goodbye to the computer department?'

So it was dismissal! Elyn tilted her head an arrogant fraction. 'Why?' she enquired coolly, and looked him squarely in the eye to read in his, not dismissal, but— as his glance went over the proud look of her, the stiff-backed trim figure she made in her well-cut jacket— something akin to admiration.

'What a blunt young woman you are!' he drawled at length, her sharp question obviously not what he was used to.

'I should be grateful that you're unfairly dismissing me?' she snapped hostilely as a flurry of anxiety made her want to shorten this interview.

But apparently, despite his remark about her saying goodbye to the computer department, dismissal was not what Max Zappelli had in mind. 'Who said anything about dismissal?' he retorted, and to her eyes he even seemed a little taken aback that such thoughts were going through her head.

'I thought...' she began, but broke off and started to prod her intelligence. 'You wish me to work in some other department?' she queried tentatively.

'To be more precise,' he said, a hint of a smile coming to his expression, 'I would be more than grateful if this afternoon you could do some work for me.'

'Oh,' she murmured, her insides, which had been twittering since Tino had put down the phone from his employer's call, now jumping all over the place.

'You *can* type?' he asked.

Solemnly Elyn stared at him. He knew perfectly well she could type. She'd like to bet that he'd been through her job application form with a fine-tooth comb! 'I'm out of practice,' she reminded him. 'The various types of computer software I use rule out the necessity for word-processing.'

'I'm sure you'll do very well,' he declared as though there was no question but that what he decreed followed. 'Unfortunately, the bilingual secretary I normally work with has gone home ill, and...'

'Felicita?' Elyn jumped in promptly as she caught his drift. 'Felicita's English is fluent. Can she not...?'

'Are you saying you prefer not to work for me?' he challenged abruptly, not so much as a hint of a smile about him now.

'No, of course not,' she was forced to reply—either that, or, she knew, run the risk of him assuring her that if she didn't want to work for him then he wouldn't dream of detaining her.

'Then allow me to proceed,' he went on coldly, and while condescending to let her know that Felicita had her hands full with her own work, he outlined the task he was working on which, in English, he wanted completing that day.

Elyn looked over the papers he showed her, which, because he must know she couldn't take shorthand, he was having to write by hand. 'You want it *all* tonight?' she asked faintly.

His answer was to lean back in his chair and to smile pleasantly. 'If it's no trouble,' he murmured.

'No trouble at all,' she replied.

'Good,' he commented, and became very businesslike, indicating a desk—on which stood a typewriter—over by a window. 'Because you will no doubt have to constantly refer to me when you cannot understand my writing, I've had a desk brought to my office.'

'I'm to work—in here?' Elyn wasn't too sure how she felt about that. She was nervous just at the thought of it, and was certain that her fingers would be all thumbs with him watching.

He nodded. 'Now...' he began, but hurriedly she interrupted him.

'May I pop back to the computer department to pick up my bag and coat?' she asked, and, when he looked a shade askance at that, 'From the look of it, I shall be here until midnight, and I should hate the department to be locked up if I have to go for it later.'

'As quickly as you can, then,' he agreed.

I'll run all the way, she felt like telling him, but, feeling rather sour with him, she adopted a sweet expression and went to find her way back to the computer department. She explained to Tino that, because their employer wanted some typing—in English—done, she would be working late, and would have to cry off their dinner arrangement.

'Are you free tomorrow evening?' he asked promptly, and suddenly Elyn wasn't so sure about such eagerness.

'Er—I'm going sightseeing in Bolzano tomorrow,' she brought out a place name that meant nothing to her, but which Felicita had said at lunchtime was worth a visit. 'I'm not sure what time I'll be back.'

'If you're not going to Bolzano with anyone, I'd very much enjoy to take you,' Tino assured her.

'Um...' she hesitated, then realised that, because she had always been so choosy about who she went out with, she might have missed out a little. Besides which, she liked Tino, and eagerness was better than indifference every time. 'That would be great!' she accepted, and when a few minutes before she'd had nothing in particular on her mind to do the following day, she arranged at what time Tino should call for her, collected her bag and coat and retraced her steps to Max Zappelli's office.

As she had suspected, she made a dreadful hash for her first two or three attempts, and rather hoped, as she binned her third attempt, that the man who was seated somewhere behind her might tell her to forget it and that he'd made a mistake in thinking she could cope—but he did no such thing. After that, though, and by forcing herself to slow down, Elyn started to make progress. And an hour later, although she wasn't breaking any records, she had picked up speed and was chugging along quite nicely.

From typing out a few handwritten letters, she went on to type a lengthy report. It was concise, and Max had a nice turn of phrase, and all at once she was starting to get deeply absorbed. In fact, so totally into what she was typing was she that she nearly jumped out of her skin when a voice suddenly spoke from behind her. 'You have no trouble in reading my writing?'

She turned in her seat to look at him, her interest so taken with what she was doing that she forgot every bit of her earlier feelings of hostility towards him. 'You must be using your best handwriting for my benefit,' she smiled, saw his glance flick to her curving lips, and turned back. Soon she was once more absorbed in the cleverness of what the sophisticated Italian had written.

Felicita came through the communicating door from her own office twice, the first time to have a discussion with her employer, and the second to wish them both, '*Buona notte.*' Elyn typed on when Felicita had gone, and finally finished everything her employer had written up for her at ten past eight that evening. He was still busily writing away behind her, but she began to hope that anything else he had could wait until Monday—with luck the person who did his bilingual work would be back by then.

But, because she'd cut her tongue out rather than admit to feeling weary, she neatened the pile of what she had typed, and swung round her typist's chair to enquire, 'Anything else?'

He looked up, stared for a moment as if appreciatively, but shook his head. 'That's it,' he replied, and his glance following hers to the paperwork before him. 'This is other work,' he offered, and with a smiling admission, 'I've had sufficient for today.'

That went for Elyn too, so she didn't argue but got up and took her typed pages over to him, and stood quietly by while he checked the first couple of pages.

'For someone who's out of practice, you've done an excellent typing job, Elyn,' he commented.

'I—found it most interesting,' she heard herself confessing, and immediately—because it sounded so like flattery—she wished she hadn't. Abruptly she went and shrugged into her coat and picked up her bag. 'I'll say g...' was as far as she got when his smile became a positive grin, a heart-stopping grin, that caused her to break off.

'Come now, Miss Talbot,' he drawled. 'You think after all your hard work I would allow you to walk home?'

'I can...'

But he was consulting his watch and, with a small exclamation in Italian, said, 'Why didn't you remind me of the time?' It was *her* fault! 'The canteen will have closed long ago,' he went on, 'and I'm starving,' he declared, and while Elyn was in the throes of doubting that he had ever eaten in the staff canteen in his life, he suddenly seemed to realise that, if he hadn't eaten, then neither had she, and, as suddenly, he asked, 'What are you doing for a meal?'

Steady, the suspicious side of Elyn warned. This man is a philanderer of the first water. Against that, though, as something closely akin to a feeling of excitement stirred in her veins, he genuinely seemed to have forgotten all about food. Good heavens, she thought, it wasn't as if he was going to run off with her, or even had designs on her! 'As yet,' she smiled, and openly revealed, 'I haven't fully loaded up my fridge, so I'll...' The sharp exclamation he made, the look that followed of a man who was regretting an oversight, caused her to falter.

'Please forgive me, Elyn. I should have arranged that you had food in your refrigerator!'

'No, you shouldn't,' she interrupted him pleasantly. And, for some unknown reason feeling that she wanted to make him feel better for what he clearly regarded as thoughtlessness, she added cheerfully, 'I can easily call in and get something on my way to the apartment.'

'Will you allow me to take you for a meal?' he asked, and when she hesitated, 'To show you truly forgive me?'

Oh, help, Elyn thought, wishing she were back in England. She could handle the situation in England. Here, common sense seemed to be slipping from her grasp. Don't be an idiot, her backbone gave her a push, what did she think was going to happen to her, for goodness' sake!

'I'm starving too!' she accepted, and shortly afterwards she was seated beside him in his Ferrari, having a private war with regard to the fact that she had accepted a date with Tino Agosta without all this soul-searching, for heaven's sake. Not that Tino was in the

same league as her employer—nor could sharing a meal
with her employer at the end of a busy day be called a
date, either.

The restaurant which Max Zappelli took her to was
smart, yet somehow managed to retain a friendly family
atmosphere. Because of her lack of Italian, Elyn was
pleased to allow her employer to choose for her.

'This is delicious,' she smiled appreciatively as she
tucked into her starter of *spaghetti alla napoletana*, which
was basically a tomato, onion and basil sauce on a bed
of spaghetti.

'You said you were starving,' Max reminded her
affably.

'You too,' she grinned, noting that he had ordered the
same for himself, but suddenly, when the corners of his
mouth picked up too, she began to feel quite mesmerised
by him. He really has a most superb mouth, she found
herself thinking, and flicked a glance upwards to his
eyes—and discovered that his glance was on her own
upward-curving mouth.

All at once, as her smile departed, so too did all hint
of a smile vanish from his mouth, and she felt tension
in the air. Solemnly they stared at one another. Then,
just when she was having trouble breathing, 'Eat!' he
commanded, and, the spell broken, Elyn looked away
from him—searching desperately for something to say
that would make nonsense of any notion he might have
gleaned that he was the cause of her breathlessness.

'Is this one of your favourite eating places, Mr
Zappelli?' she enquired off the top of her head.

'One of them,' he agreed urbanely, and added, 'Call
me Max, Elyn—I promise I don't bite!'

Had he guessed, could he see, that she was nervous
of him? No, not nervous, she changed her mind—wary
of him; wary, that was it. 'I'm sure you don't,' she replied evenly, and to show just how unaffected by him

she was, 'Max,' she added lightly, and took a sip of a
most pleasant-tasting wine.

The pasta course was followed by an equally delicious
dish of *pesce in casseruola*, a fish casserole, with prawns,
a few other types of fish, a few strips of carrot, a few
fennel seeds—and a gorgeous flavour.

'Is the dish to your liking?' the host enquired.

'English cooking is going to seem tame after this,' she
laughed. 'Talking of England,' she went on, finding that
somehow, something was pushing her to talk, 'are you
due to pay Pinwich a visit soon?'

'You're homesick?' he enquired.

'That wasn't what I asked,' she prevaricated. Just now,
right at this minute, she didn't know what she was.

It was his turn to laugh lightly, just as if he found her
congenial company, she thought headily, but she kept
her expression even, while she waited for an answer to
her question. 'England is not on my immediate agenda,'
Max replied at last. 'In fact I'm desk-bound for the next
two weeks, I believe.'

'Then England?' she guessed.

'Then Rome,' he said, and for no reason, perhaps it
was the charm of his delivery, Elyn wanted to laugh
again. Instead she concentrated on her *pesce in
casseruola*.

When the time came for her to order a sweet, she had
little room left. 'Perhaps a small ice-cream,' she replied
to her host's coaxing.

'How are you enjoying the computer section?' Max
asked over coffee.

'Tremendously,' she answered and, telling the truth
and shaming the devil, 'As you realised, and I've now
seen for myself, my computer skills were seriously in need
of an update,' she confessed.

'It's very honest of you to admit it,' he remarked, and
suddenly that word 'honest' seemed to be suspended
in the air.

Elyn had enjoyed her meal with Max Zappelli. But while something in her at the moment wanted to challenge him about having doubts about her honesty in another area, another part of her suddenly didn't want this pleasant interlude to end on a sorry note. Which she knew full well it would if he started accusing her of design-lifting again.

'Tino Agosta is an excellent teacher,' she rattled out of a thin nowhere.

'So I believe,' Max agreed coolly, and Elyn knew then that it wasn't so much that he didn't want her to bring Tino into the conversation, as that he was remembering the business of Brian Cole's design that had gone missing.

That, as far as she could see, was that. No way was she grovelling to this man with protestations of her innocence. She stood up. 'Thank you very much for my dinner,' she said politely, and as he, getting over his surprise, got to his feet too, 'I'll make my own way home,' she informed him.

For a moment he just stood and stared at her. Then suddenly the sauciest grin lit his features and, not deigning to argue, he mocked, 'You don't even know how to get there from here,' and something rose up in Elyn at his grin, his manner, that caused her to forget entirely that he had ever in any way offended her. He called for her coat, and held on to her with one hand while he put some lire down on the table for their meal with the other.

'*Grazie, signore,*' the head waiter beamed as he went with them to the door and held it open for them.

By the time Max drew up outside her apartment, Elyn's equilibrium was fully restored. She turned in her seat, intending to thank him, nicely this time, for her dinner— then discovered that he had come round to her door and was opening it.

Her 'thank you' was again put on ice when he went into the building with her and, exchanging greetings with Uberto as they went, escorted her over to the lift. Elyn half turned, ready again with her thanks when the lift came—and Max got in with her.

She was feeling a good deal bemused by the time they arrived at the apartment door and he held out his hand for the key. Witlessly, she handed it over, and he unlocked the door. But then, as she crossed over the threshold, he held back.

She turned and looked at him. 'Do I get invited in, Elyn?' he asked softly.

Oh, heavens, she panicked, she should say no, or trot out something trite like, you were here last Wednesday, don't tell me you've forgotten what it looks like so soon. But she didn't say anything of the sort. Max wasn't some callow youth who would push his way in—he was waiting for her permission.

'I haven't any strong Italian coffee I can offer you,' she murmured, and turned round. Max followed her in.

'Forget the coffee,' he stated. 'I won't be staying more than a few minutes.' She should have felt relieved that all he had wanted to do was to see her safely inside before he left—but she wasn't. 'How did you get to work this morning?' he enquired casually as, flicking light switches on as they went, they halted in the centre of her sitting-room. And as Elyn blinked at the unexpectedness of that question, 'Felicita mentioned that you didn't want her to pick you up any more.'

'I hope I was more polite than that!' Elyn murmured, dropping down her bag and undoing her coat. 'Felicita had to go out of her way to pick me up on Thursday, and although she said she didn't mind at all, I—um—rather like to walk.'

'Are you always this proud?' Max questioned.

'Proud?' she repeated, and found he had come a step or two closer and that she was looking up into his warm dark gaze. She took a nervous step towards the door, as though to show him out. 'I—er—like to pay my way,' she agreed, then burst out laughing as it struck her that he had paid for her meal, and turned to look at him. 'Which reminds me. Thank you, sincerely, for my dinner.'

She wasn't sure what she expected him to say then, but as he looked down into her green eyes, suddenly he seemed arrested. 'You really are stunningly beautiful,' he told her, just as if the words were pulled from him and wouldn't be held in. Elyn was still staring up at him dumbstruck when, 'What in hell's wrong with Englishmen?' he asked softly, and came yet another step nearer.

'Nothing's wrong with them,' she defended, and tried to make out what he was getting at. He took the other step that brought him so that their bodies were almost touching, and she didn't back away—indeed, she felt as though she could not move an inch. 'Oh!' she exclaimed as it suddenly came to her that he must mean, what was the matter with Englishmen that at twenty-two she was still a virgin. 'I don't date all that much,' she found her voice, husky though it was, to tell him.

'It can't be for want of offers,' Max commented, his hands coming up to take her arms in a gentle hold.

'I've—er—been in charge, sort of—at work, I mean—for my stepfather. It's—er——' oh, heavens, just his touch was making her brainless! 'It's not a nine-to-five job—being in charge, I mean,' she added. 'There's n-no point in making a date when you don't know if you can keep it.'

'I know what you mean,' he murmured, moving just that small fraction. Then all at once, while giving her all the time in the world to pull away, he gathered her in his arms, then slowly placed his mouth over hers.

An 'Oh!' escaped her when he broke that so beautiful, so gentle kiss, and her lips were still forming a welcoming 'O' when he claimed them again, his kiss more intense this time as his arms beneath her coat pulled her closer to him.

Quite what was happening to her, Elyn didn't stop to analyse. All she knew, as her arms went up and around him, was that never had she been kissed like this before, and, as a fire started to flicker into flames of a burning need for him, she didn't want him to stop.

Nor did he stop. Somehow she was divested of her coat and, with their bodies moulded to each other as he pressed her to him, again and again he kissed her.

Passion soared between them, and Elyn was mindless to all and everything when she found she was lying in the luxury of the couch with him, his body over hers pressing her down, down, down, into its welcoming confines.

Why alarm bells should choose to go off in her head then, when up until that moment they had chosen to remain stubbornly silent, was a mystery to her. But as the glorious touch of Max's hands doing mind-bending, mind-blowing things to the bare smooth silk of her shoulder beneath her bra strap suddenly let loose a moment of a different awareness, so as Max broke his kiss Elyn took a gulp of air—and with it, a trace of sanity.

'Max, no!' she cried. 'Oh, Max, I...' Helplessly she struggled, but she was on fire for him, and that trace of sanity swiftly departed, and she was about to contradict her 'No' with an 'Oh, Max yes!' when the pressure of his body over hers eased, and he rolled away from her. But to have him sitting on the couch, his back towards her, his arms no longer around her, was not what she wanted at all! 'Max, I...' she began.

'A moment, *cara*,' he cut in. 'Give me a minute, please.'

I want you back, back here with me, she wanted to plead. But, aflame with need for him as she was, as he had observed, she had pride, and something extra, and the words to tell him of her need refused to come.

Though it seemed that he was aware of her need anyway, for, having taken the moments he required to gain his own self-control, he enquired stiffly, 'You are all right, Elyn?'

His stiff tone was just what she needed. 'Yes, thank you,' she said coolly—and was not at all surprised when, pausing only to pick up his jacket, without so much as a backward glance he got up and walked out of the apartment—to leave her staring stunned after him.

Yes, thank you, she had said in answer to his, 'Are you all right?'. But there was no yes, thank you about it, and she was most definitely not all right. Because she, stupid, ridiculous poor idiot, had gone and done the unthinkable—she had fallen for a most unsuitable man.

CHAPTER FIVE

AFTER a fitful night, Elyn was up early on Saturday morning. She had never felt less like sightseeing, and sorely wished she had never agreed to let Tino Agosta take her to Bolzano. But when the hall porter rang and speaking slowly said something about 'Signor Agosta', she was ready.

'*Grazie*,' she replied and, presuming that Tino had arrived to call for her ten minutes early, she donned a jacket, picked up her shoulder bag and left the apartment.

'Good morning, Elyn.' Tino's greeting was warm as she stepped out of the lift.

'Hello, Tino,' she found a smile in return, and minutes later they were in his car and making for the resort in the north-eastern part of Italy.

She'd had no idea, when she'd said she thought she would go to Bolzano today, that Bolzano lay in the Dolomites, or that it was about a two-hour drive away. Two hours was much too long to sit idle—she needed to be up and doing. She had thought for most of the night, and didn't want space to think any more.

'You're very quiet,' Tino remarked as they sped along.

'I'm sorry,' she apologised. 'I thought I'd leave you to concentrate on your driving.' When had lying ever come so easily? It never had, came back the answer. Love had made a liar of her.

She did not want to be in love, though. Not with Max Zappelli, she didn't. He might have had her half swooning for him last night, but in the cold light of day it was clear that even philanderers had some standards.

In the cold light of day it was patently obvious that, even though there was no mistaking that he had desired her, her small 'no' of protest had given him a moment to pause, and to recall that she was, or could be, a thief.

That Max had more about him than to want to bed someone he thought capable of stealing from his company was of no consolation. Because when the time came, when surely if there was any justice it must, that the real taker of those designs was discovered, it still left him as a number one womaniser. And, remembering her mother's pain at the hands of one such, remembering her stepsister's heartbreak on so many occasions, Elyn had no room in her life for such a man. Reality gave a distinctive nasty laugh—as if Max Zappelli, with all he'd got going for him, not to mention the beautiful creatures she'd seen photographed on his arm, would have room in his life for her!

'We may have a problem parking, but we shall see,' Tino broke through her thoughts, causing her to realise that not only had they arrived at their destination, but also that she must have exchanged a dozen or so pleasantries with him on the journey without being fully aware of it.

At that moment she brought herself up short. Tino deserved better than that, for goodness' sake! Good manners if nothing else decreed that, since she had accepted his offer, she should make some effort to enjoy it.

'We're lucky with the weather,' she remarked blithely, as they stepped out into brilliant sunshine.

Tino smiled, gave her a look as though to say he thought himself lucky, and suggested, 'Shall we have coffee?'

'Can we have it outside?' she asked.

'Of course,' he said at once, and shortly afterwards they were seated in the Piazza Walther Platz, drinking coffee and being warmed by the sun, which was surprisingly strong for February.

'Is the square named after anyone in particular?' Elyn asked, determined, now she'd been prodded by good manners, to show an interest.

'Walther von der Vogelweid,' Tino told her, and pointing to a marble statue across the square to the right of them, 'He was a poet of the Middle Ages, and held in very great esteem.'

If Tino had been mugging up on Bolzano before he had called for her, then in Elyn's view he had done brilliantly, for as they moved from the café and wandered around, he seemed able to answer every one of her questions.

The novelist and dramatist Goethe had found the outdoor fruit market most impressive, he told her as they strolled over cobbled streets and past the bronze Neptune Fountain, and through the colourful fruit market.

'You must be hungry, Elyn!' Tino exclaimed suddenly after they had been walking around for quite some while.

She wasn't, but because she had an idea that Tino was, she said, 'I could do with a little something,' and went with him to a small restaurant, ate a plate of tagliatelle with ham and tomatoes, and tried desperately hard not to think how last night she had shared a meal with Max.

Lunch over, Tino confessed to an interest in visiting the museum. 'What are we waiting for?' she teased, and went with him with an outward show of not having a thing on her mind but the prehistoric archaeological finds they would see when they got there.

Time was getting on by the time they came out. 'Now, what shall we see?' Tino asked.

'Er—do you think we should think about getting back to Verona now?' she suggested.

'Of course. But only if you will have the dinner with me which you had to cancel last night.'

It was the earnestness of his smile that touched her. 'I'd be delighted,' she accepted, when what she more particularly wanted was that this day would end so that she could go and lock herself in the apartment and bury herself in solitude.

As matters evolved, she was eventually able to plead that it had been a long, though very enjoyable day, and Tino, like the very nice person he was, took her home at around ten o'clock.

'I hope you have enjoyed your time with me?' he questioned, as they stood by his car prior to her going in.

'Very much,' she answered him warmly, then saw his kiss coming and took an evasive step back to hold out her hand. 'Thank you so much, Tino,' she said, and liked him a lot when he didn't force the issue, but shook hands.

'Are you free tomorrow?' he asked hopefully.

'I'm afraid not,' she said regretfully.

'Until Monday, then,' he smiled.

'Until Monday,' she said, and went indoors.

Sunday had to be got through first, and at one stage Elyn got so churned up inside, her thoughts, all centred on Max Zappelli, chasing one after the other, that in desperation, needing to speak to someone and so get him out of her head, she phoned her mother.

'I've been wondering how you've been getting on!' Ann Pillinger exclaimed, sounding very pleased to hear her.

'Heavens, did I have a lot to learn!' And how! Firstly how to get something else on her brain other than Max. 'How is everybody?' she asked cheerfully.

'Sam's the same as ever, Loraine—well, you know Loraine, sighing about the place doing her Dying Swan act, and Guy,' Ann ended crossly, 'is being *particularly* difficult.'

'Oh, dear,' Elyn sympathised. 'He has had a nasty shock,' she attempted to excuse him.

'We've *all* had a nasty shock!' her mother refused to excuse him.

'I expect he's getting a little bit bored,' Elyn tried again.

'Well, I wish he'd go and be bored somewhere else. That young man is becoming exceedingly tiresome!'

'Well, how are you?' Elyn asked, determined to be bright.

'With my overdraft at the bank going up and up, you need to ask?'

'What do you need an overdraft for?' Elyn panicked, her deep-rooted hatred of debt rocketing.

'If you think I'm going to go to Sam every time I need a new pair of tights, you can think again!' her mother replied stoutly.

Elyn ultimately came off the phone having soothed her mother's ruffled feathers, but knowing that it was wanting more than a mere new pair of tights to wear that was causing her mother's overdraft to rise.

She half wished she hadn't telephoned—it hadn't occurred to her that her mother would be getting credit from the bank, but she supposed it should have done. Oh, lord, it didn't look as if her car money would last much longer!

By Monday morning, when Elyn left her apartment to walk to Zappelli Internazionale, however, there was no room in her head for her family's financial affairs. Would she see Max? How on earth was she supposed to act?

She returned home that night in glum spirits. She was so confused by then that she didn't know if she was glad or sorry she had not so much as clapped eyes on the man who, sneakily, while she wasn't looking—when she would have said all the odds were against it—had crept in and stolen her heart.

By Tuesday she was experiencing some desperate kind of feelings, and knew a most urgent need to see him. But, as on the previous evening, she returned to her apartment that night without having caught so much as a glimpse of him.

I don't care, I don't care, she tried to tell herself on Wednesday. She was in one of the corridors on her way back to her office after lunch, however, when she suddenly caught sight of him coming her way, and as her heart went into overdrive, she knew how completely ridiculous that was—she did care, oh, so much! Her heart was drumming nineteen to the dozen before he was anywhere near. When he drew level and actually halted, she could barely breathe.

'You're enjoying your work, Miss Talbot?' he paused to enquire. The 'Miss Talbot', even without his cool tone, was sufficient to tell her that, *still* believing her to be a crook, he was not only regretting having fed her on Friday night but was positively loathing the fact that he had ever taken her in his arms and begun to make love to her.

'Loving it!' she answered coldly, and somehow even managed to stare up into his lofty dark gaze before— she with a tilt of her chin and he with a curt nod—they walked on in opposite directions.

Damn him, she fumed. Him with his dismissive nods— who the hell did he think he was!

'I don't suppose you would like to come out for a meal tonight?' asked Tino, having asked her on Monday and Tuesday without success but chancing it again while the others were not back from lunch and there was no one with a smattering of English to hear.

The way Elyn was feeling just then, she'd have gone out with the devil himself rather than spend that night stuck in the apartment with that disbelieving monster again the sole occupant of her thoughts. 'Only if you let me pay,' she told Tino.

At once a smile lit his face, though it seemed he wasn't too thrilled at the idea of her paying for the meal. 'This is an English custom?' he enquired.

This is my way of saying that I want to be friends with you—platonic friends, she wanted to tell him, but settled for, 'In these days of equality, I don't see why you should pay for my dinner tonight as well as last Saturday.'

Elyn dined with Tino that night and found him as uncomplicated as ever, but when she returned to her apartment he was not the man who dominated her thoughts.

She did not see Max again that week, and, having declined Tino's offer to take her sightseeing anywhere she would like to go that weekend, she spent Saturday sightseeing alone, around Verona. But even the mighty and majestic amphitheatre could not dispel Max from her thoughts for very long.

As she had on the previous Sunday, it was with a despairing feeling of wanting to be the person she had been before she had fallen in love with Max that she again put through a call to her mother.

The call followed the same pattern as her previous one. 'Everyone all right?' Elyn asked.

'It's snowing, but Sam's starting to think about money,' her mother reported. Elyn took that as a good sign. 'Loraine has brought home yet another unsuitable type—lord only knows where she finds them—and, give three cheers, Guy is looking round for a job.'

'Oh, that's great!' Elyn exclaimed, and rang off feeling much more cheered than she had the last time. Bless them, they'd all had a nasty shock, as her mother had said last week, but—and although it had taken time— it now looked as if they might be getting over it.

The next morning Elyn went to Zappelli Internazionale to start another week, and to wonder how much longer she would be working in Italy—and how she would feel when the possibility of accidentally bumping into Max in some corridor became even more remote. A sinking feeling smote her at that thought, but it had to be faced. Tino was thorough in his training, and because of that, her progress wasn't so fast as perhaps it might have been. They were now working as well as training, but possibly around the Easter Max had spoken of it would all be ended, and she would return to England.

'Good morning, Tino!' she exclaimed brightly when she went in.

'You'll have dinner with me this evening?' he jumped straight in, and Elyn laughed. He wasn't Max, but he was nice.

'Tomorrow,' she answered, and as the others of the section drifted in, with Tino's help, she got down to some work.

She half dreaded, half hoped that she might see something of Max that day, but she saw nothing of him on Monday or Tuesday either, and she prepared to go out with Tino on Tuesday evening, giving herself the sternest lecture. The bracing theme of which was, why was she wasting her time pining over a man like Max when, save for a lapse when his philandering self had gone on automatic pilot, he was barely aware of her existence?

Dinner with Tino was friendly and pleasant, and she was pleased at how well they got on. Though she owned to feeling a little awkward when, presumably feeling the same, he suddenly leaned across the table and blurted out, 'I have wondered if you will come away and share the weekend with me?'

'Oh, I don't know about that, Tino,' she began to back away fast, wondering when she had ever given him the impression that she was more interested in him than being just friends. 'I like you, but——'

'Oh!' he interrupted. 'I have asked you badly. You shall have your own room, of course,' he hurried on. 'I just thought you might like to come with me to ski.'

A smile touched her mouth. What a sweetie he was! 'I can't ski,' she told him, and saw a look of relief cross his features that he had not offended her.

'I will teach you,' he asserted, and suddenly Elyn quite liked the idea. Perhaps an overdose of energetic activity was what she needed. She didn't fancy another weekend like the last one, that was for sure.

'Where will we find snow?' she asked, and saw him start to beam when it looked as if she was on the way to accepting.

'High in the mountains—in the Dolomites,' he told her, and the rest of the meal was spent in discussion of the proposed weekend in a place called Cavalese.

Elyn felt more cheered than she had of late as she made her way to Zappelli Internazionale the next morning. She was going to be more positive, she decided. After hitting the depths last weekend, she was going to put all that behind her. Max Zappelli wasn't for her, and if he was, she wouldn't want him, she decided firmly—then saw him, and promptly went weak at the knees.

Oh, grief, he was coming from the firm's car park to the left, she was on the centre path, and they were both making for the wide front entrance of Zappelli's—their paths were bound to collide! Knowing that short of doing a swift about-turn, which pride decreed was entirely out of the question, she could not avoid him, Elyn struggled hard to keep her pace even.

Any positive feelings she had earlier determined upon were long gone, though, when as their steps converged, he greeted her crisply from his lofty height, 'Good morning.'

'Good morning,' she responded politely, if stiffly, and thought, as they neared the entrance of the building, that that would be the sum total of their conversation.

But, as Max stretched out a hand and seemed about to pull back one of the double doors, 'You're not finding your time in Italy too lonely, I hope?' he enquired, as any employer might—and that made her mad.

He had kissed her, dammit, made her feel as though she wasn't just any old employee! 'Thinking of sending me back?' she sent him a hostile look to challenge.

He didn't like her challenging tone, she could see that from the icy way his dark eyes stared down into her furious green ones. 'You'll go back when I say!' he retorted, and, pulling open the door, he exploded with something very Italian before, his tone changing, he added silkily, 'I shouldn't want you staying in nights, or...'

Swine! she raged. 'There's no fear of that,' she cut in, at pains to let him know she wasn't staying in nights on account of *him*. 'When I'm not in Bolzano...'

'You've been to Bolzano?' he sliced in aggressively, and before she could draw breath, he demanded, 'Who with?'

'Who with?' she echoed.

'You haven't your own transport!' he rapped.

'No, but I do have friends!' she snapped, then she put her head in the air and sailed through the door. Who the hell did he think he was? Him and his sarcastic, 'I shouldn't want you staying in nights', just as though she had a face like the back of a bus and no offers!

By lunchtime she'd calmed down. By that evening, having gone through their conversation many times, she had thought of a dozen so much sharper things she could have said. Among them that on Friday she was going off to a place called Cavalese for the weekend with 'a friend'—how about that for being lonely?

'I have reserved the rooms for us in the hotel,' Tino told her in an undertone at work the next morning. 'I was very lucky,' he went on happily. 'They were fully booked, but had just received a cancellation.'

'Lovely!' she smiled enthusiastically, determined never to sink down to the depths ever again.

She had a few bits of shopping to do at lunchtime, so she popped out for them first, then went to the firm's canteen. 'Elyn, there's a seat here!' Felicita Rocca called, and Elyn—smiling her 'thanks but no, thanks' to a man from her own office who had tried to date her but who she knew was married and who was now pointing to an empty place at his table—went over and sat at Felicita's table. 'How is the computer-room?' Felicita asked.

'Fabulous!' Elyn enthused, and stamped down hard on any question that arose about Felicita's office, and the man she worked for. 'Have you worked here long?' she enquired instead, and from there they exchanged a few more pleasantries, then somehow got on to the subject of their families.

'Have you heard from your family since you have been in Italy?' Felicita asked in some concern.

'I spoke with my mother on the phone last Sunday, actually,' Elyn told her, and, suddenly remembering, 'It was snowing then—in England, I mean,' she laughed, and thinking of snow, she suddenly found she was telling Felicita about her forthcoming skiing trip.

'You ski?'

'No,' Elyn laughed. 'That's what worries me! Though Tino says I can get fixed up with boots and skis when I get there, and he'll teach me the rest.'

They chatted for a little while longer, then Elyn looked at her watch, and so too did Felicita. 'I must go,' she said, and, having finished her snack, Elyn got up with her.

'Have a good time in Cavalese!' Felicita wished her as they parted.

'Thanks,' said Elyn, and went thoughtfully back to her own office to wonder if she so much wanted Max to know that she wouldn't be stuck in the apartment staring at her four walls this coming weekend that she had told Felicita about her plans in the hope that she would pass them on to him. I'm just not that devious, she denied. But then she hadn't been a fibber either, until she had fallen in love.

Any feelings of 'so there, Max Zappelli, I'm going to be so busy this weekend I won't have a chance to be lonely!' evaporated into nothing when she reached the office the next morning. As ever, Tino was first in.

'I am so sorry, Elyn,' he began straight away, and swiftly, referring to the memo he had in his hands, 'I found this on my desk this morning. I am invited to attend a special tutorial in Milano tomorrow. Can you understand, Elyn, that it is a compliment to me, and would greatly enhance my knowledge, if I could go?'

'But you must certainly go,' she smiled.

'You don't mind about my not being able to take you?'

'Of course not!' she insisted, and was heartily glad then that Max did not know of her trip to Cavalese. She didn't want him asking, not that he would, how her skiing trip had gone, only to have to tell him it hadn't.

'You are very kind,' Tino told her gratefully. 'But I was sure that you would be—which is why I telephoned my sister five minutes ago.'

'Your sister?' Elyn queried, trying to get on to his wavelength.

'Diletta is driving in the direction of Cavalese on Friday to stay the weekend with her fiancé's family. She will be very much pleased to have your company on the drive.'

'Oh, but...'

'Please, Elyn,' Tino cut in. 'I promised you would ski, and I feel unhappy to break my word. But...'

Ten minutes later they got down to some work, with Elyn unsure that she wanted to go to this place Cavalese now, but with Diletta Agosta's telephone number in her purse. His sister, so Tino had said, would be home from work at six and would like to leave Verona before seven, and would like Elyn to confirm whether or not she would like to take advantage of a lift. Meantime Tino had been

through to the Hotel Cavalese, and had cancelled just
one of the rooms he had reserved.

Had Elyn still been undecided what to do—Verona or
Cavalese for the weekend—then the matter was decided
for her when, just as she was leaving the building that
night, the tall and superbly fit figure of Max Zappelli
fell into step with her.

Just to see him made adrenalin spurt through her veins,
and she could only thank her pride that somehow she
managed to maintain a calm outer appearance. 'How
are you getting along in computer land?' he enquired
evenly, briefcase in hand, as they approached the double
doors.

'Quite well, I think,' she murmured politely. 'Tino
Agosta is a very good teacher.'

She thought her employer grunted something in Italian
that sounded a shade tetchy, but realised she was mistaken when, his tone quite pleasant, indeed silky almost,
he commented 'Good,' and, reaching the doors, stood
back and held one open for her to go through. 'As usual,
you are not going to be lonely in a foreign land this
weekend?'

Was he being sarcastic? Did he think, despite her efforts to disabuse him of the idea, that she had nothing
of a social nature going on in her life? It was, if nothing
else, a point of honour that she set him straight about
that issue without delay. 'Oh, I'm sure I shan't be lonely,'
she trotted out brightly as she went out into the cold
night air and he followed. 'There are bound to be loads
of skiers where I'm going.' With that she added a cool,
'Goodnight, Mr Zappelli,' and went smartly down the
path. Somehow, though, she had the oddest notion that
he was still standing there watching her—she had no intention of turning round to find out for sure!

Diletta Agosta was a bubbly woman who was as
outward-going as her brother was quiet. Her English was
not as good as his, but on the two-and-a-half-hour drive

to Cavalese they managed to communicate quite well. And it was with a chirpy '*Ciao*, Elyn, I see you half an hour after four o'clock on Sunday,' that Diletta dropped her off at her hotel and plunged expertly straight into the middle of the chaotic weekend tourist traffic.

'Ah, Signorina Talbot!' the man on Reception welcomed Elyn, his eyes enjoying her beauty as she signed in. 'You will want the dinner, *no*?'

'*Si, grazie*,' Elyn smiled, and followed the young porter who with her bag and room key was heading for her room.

Her hotel was clean and comfortable, and the food was good. Elyn put Max Zappelli as far from her thoughts as she could, and decided she would treat the whole weekend as one big adventure.

With that in mind, she firmly ousted Max from her head when she awoke on Saturday morning and, with no Tino there to teach her to ski, breakfasted on ham and cheese, then donned warm clothing and her snow-boots, and decided to take a walk around town.

Cavalese, she discovered, was not an over-large town, and she window-shopped up one side of a street and then the other. This was a holiday, she told herself, she could do what she liked. She went into a nearby café and ordered coffee, promising herself that she would call back in the afternoon and treat herself to one of those delicious-looking pastries.

Her coffee finished, she set off again exploring the town that was dominated by snowy mountains. It was around lunchtime, though, that she found she was in the vicinity of where the cable car departed from. To her mind it seemed logical that there would be an establishment of some sort up on the mountains where she could get something to eat. Places, too, where she could perhaps walk around a little as well. Elyn decided to go in for a little more adventure.

Having purchased a ski-pass, she discovered that her ride up Alpe Cermis involved two cable cars. She presumed that must be because that particular alp was so steep, and halfway up at a station she exchanged one cable car for another.

A feeling of pleasure filled her as, vacating the second car, she wandered away from her forty or so fellow passengers, and, breathing in the pure crisp air, took in the delight of the view.

There were no skiers where she was, and she strolled on upwards and looked across to see that the ski area was quite crowded. There was a chair-lift, she noticed, so presumably the more accomplished skiers took that and skied down by more complicated routes.

She spotted a restaurant and spent a pleasant half-hour there with lasagne and coffee. When thoughts of Max started to bombard her head again, she decided to take a walk around. It was still crowded, though and, being a nature-lover, she decided to wander over to the opposite and less populated side to take a look at some stately pines.

Once she had gained the spot she was making for, there seemed to be no one about. Somehow she was sure she was still on the part where it was permitted to walk, though, and after walking on a little she suddenly spotted a tree that had separated itself from the others and, perhaps because of it, seemed to stand petrified.

For a long time she admired it from a distance, and then nothing would do but that she had to walk over to it and study the snowy icicles that festooned it.

Well, did you ever see anything so amazing? she wondered, fascinated by the tree that was green and alive despite its mantle of hard ice and snow. She was just beginning to wish she had her camera with her, and took several paces out into the clearing for another angle of it when some sound caught her ears. Attracted by the sound, she turned her head and looked to her right—

and froze. No! screamed her head, but as alarm shot through her and she realised that she had just stepped out on to the ski-run, so she knew, as a figure dressed completely in black hurtled straight for her, that there was no way he could avoid a collision.

Totally stunned, she stood there not knowing which way to jump. Then whoosh!—the skier, by some super-human effort, had twisted to the left and, horror of horrors, he was over, in a heap, his skis going one way, he the other.

'Oh, I'm sorry, so sorry!' Elyn cried as she raced as fast as she could over to where he lay. He wasn't moving but lay still, his face turned from her. Desperately she looked around. Why, when there had been masses of people about, was there no one about in this area! 'Are you all right?' she asked frantically, and had never felt so relieved when suddenly, winded still, his head bent, he moved to a sitting position. 'Are you all right?' she repeated, desperately wishing she knew more than the smattering of Italian that she had picked up in the last few weeks.

'I don't know yet!' the man said in English—and she knew that voice!

Apprehension, fear, disbelief—not to mention a flut-tering of joy—all mingled. Elyn stared at the man, not believing any of this. He was wearing dark impenetrable sunglasses, but as she watched he pulled off his ski-hat. His hair was dark. He lifted his head, pulled his strong firm chin out of the folds of his ski-jacket. She knew that firm chin too—even if she was still not believing the evidence of her eyes. But when finally he stretched up a hand and removed his sunglasses to reveal a pair of dark penetrating eyes—dark eyes which she knew and loved—she just had to gasp out loud.

'You!' escaped her on something of a squeak. 'What are you doing here?'

There was no mistaking who he was then, for he was all arrogant and aggressive, and so much the man she knew as, 'Trying to keep out of your way without breaking my bloody neck!' Max Zappelli roared in no uncertain fashion.

CHAPTER SIX

'OH, MAX!' Elyn exclaimed, so shaken she had no chance to keep the concern out of her voice. 'Are you hurt? Can I help?'

'You don't think you've done enough?' he growled, his fierce dark eyes fixed on her stunned green ones—if he was recalling that the last time she had spoken with him she had called him Mr Zappelli, there was nothing in his look to give that away.

'I'm sorry,' she gulped agitatedly.

'So you should be!' he grunted.

Elyn took that on the chin. It was clear now that he had come down on one of the fastest runs and had never expected anyone to be so idiotic as to be standing there slap-bang in the middle of it.

'Can you get up? Can you stand?' she asked anxiously.

'Go and get my skis,' he ordered, and Elyn, glad to be able to do something, went willingly.

He was still in possession of his ski-sticks, and with the use of them had managed to get to his feet by the time she returned with his skis. 'Do you want to put them on?' she asked.

'I think not,' he said curtly—and she knew that he *had* hurt himself.

'Are you with friends?' she asked as it quickly occurred to her that she might need some help in getting him down the mountain. Though as she realised that he could well have been skiing with any one of the lovely females she had seen him pictured with, jealousy plunged a knife into her heart, and she felt an aversion to having that question answered. 'Sh-shall I get the—er—blood wagon, I think it's called?' she asked when he hadn't deigned to answer her other question anyway—she couldn't remember seeing one, but surely there had to be a first aid post somewhere.

'There's no need for that!' he snarled shortly, arrogantly, and all at once Elyn knew that, even though he might be hurting like the very devil, Max Zappelli, a very proud man, absolutely abhorred fuss.

'Very well,' she said quietly. 'But I do think it would be a good idea if we got you down off this mountain.' His eyebrows ascended at that 'we', but he said nothing, so Elyn guessed he was in agreement that it might be an idea if they made for the cable car. 'You can lean on me if it's of any help,' she offered, still feeling mortified that through her ignorance about the ways of the ski-paths, anyone, let alone the man she loved, could well have ended up with a broken neck.

Her whole body felt alive, though, when Max manoeuvred himself round and placed an arm about her shoulder and they set off.

Their progress to the cable car station was slow. Max insisted on carrying his skis, and even though Elyn knew that he was in pain, because of his mammoth pride, she had to let him.

'Not much further now,' she remarked encouragingly as they went slowly downwards and began to mingle with the masses enjoying a Saturday afternoon of sport. Really, she fretted, as with Max's arm about her they made for the cable car, he might be hurting like hell, but apart from the barest traces of a limp—his right foot, she rather thought—anyone would be hard put to it to spot that he had injured himself.

Stubborn, brave, proud darling, she thought tenderly when, having at last made it to the first cable car, they stood close waiting for it to start off. She looked up at him, wanting to check that he was all right—and found that he was looking straight down into her eyes.

'You didn't hurt *yourself*?' he enquired urgently, and Elyn could only love him the more. She guessed then that her eyes must have been moist from the sensitivity of her feelings, but the fact that he could forget his own pain and sound so concerned about her made her want to weep.

She didn't weep, of course—she had pride too. Pride that he should never guess just what, with a few enquiring kind words, he could do to her. 'Not in the slightest!' she assured him brightly—and received a grunt for an answer.

Then the cable car started up and, save for his arm, still round her shoulders, holding her more firmly—supporting her this time, holding her steady when the cable car jumped a little as they passed over a pylon—there was no more communication between them, even when they exchanged one cable car for another.

They reached the bottom and had left the cable car and were walking through the covered entrance when Elyn spotted a wide window ledge. 'If you'd like to sit there,' she suggested, indicating the low ledge, 'I'll go and see about getting you a taxi.'

Her mind was racing on to wonder if she would get her head bitten off if she dared to further suggest to this proud man that he have that right foot checked over at a hospital when, ignoring her first suggestion, he informed her coolly, 'My car's outside,' and with his arm still about her shoulders he propelled her forward and out to the car parking area.

Elyn saw the Ferrari almost straight away, albeit it now had a ski-rack fitted to it. But as they went over to it she began to get more and more anxious about Max. For, away from other eyes, his limp seemed to her to become more pronounced.

'Do you—er—think that maybe a—doctor should take a look at you?' she enquired when at his car he racked his skis, then opened up the boot.

'No,' he clipped, 'I don't.'

Count ten, Elyn, she told herself when his tone and his manner started to niggle her. He's in pain, she reminded herself—and felt dreadful for having even felt a moment's crossness with him.

'Here,' he rapped, and limping round to the driver's door, he unlocked it and instructed, 'Sit there.'

At that point Elyn experienced a decided aversion to being bossed about by him. But she bit it down. 'Very well,' she replied calmly, and in the circumstances, rather than give him more hassle, she sat sideways in the driver's seat, her feet on the outside of the car, ready to assist him in when needed.

She had presumed he had opened the boot ready to exchange his ski footwear for some ordinary shoes, but discovered that she was wrong on two counts, because it seemed he had decided to change later. For all at once he closed the boot and, apparently not needing her assistance, limped round to the passenger's side of the car, got in—and closed the door!

Elyn slewed round in her seat, giving him a surprised look. But as she stared at him, wondering what they did now, to her utter amazement, not to say horror, Max did no more than stretch out a hand and made to pass the car keys over to her. And, while she was still staring at him trying to deny the messages her brain was trying to tell her, 'Shut your door—and drive,' he instructed.

'*Drive*!' she echoed, not believing it for a moment. A Ferrari, for heaven's sake! He'd got to be joking!

He didn't look as if he was joking though. 'Drive!' he barked.

Damn you, she fumed, and didn't care a button how much he hurt then as *her* pride spiralled upwards. She was not feeling at all well disposed towards him as she snatched the keys from him, rammed them in the ignition and sat for a few moments studying the controls.

Then, praying that he wouldn't answer 'Home' which she knew to be somewhere between Bergamo airport and Verona, she asked, 'Where to?' through clenched teeth.

'I've borrowed a friend's chalet for the weekend; it's uphill on the outskirts of Cavalese,' he told her. 'I'll give you directions as we go.'

Elyn didn't wait for anything else but, grabbing at courage while she was still angry enough not to care, she turned the key in the ignition—and found the Ferrari was a much easier car to drive than her own car had been.

It was not a very long drive, however, and inside ten minutes she was pulling up outside the single-storeyed chalet. 'Hang on, I'll come round and give you a hand,' she said as she cut the engine and left the driver's seat.

Max already had the passenger door open by the time she got there, but he seemed glad of her shoulder to lean on as she helped him up the drive, up the steps and on to the half-closed-in timbered veranda of the building.

'I'll take my boots off here,' he declared, and lowered his length on to a bench and first of all took off his left boot. Elyn was hovering anxiously near him and took the boot from him. Heavens, it weighed a ton! How on earth did they manage to walk in them, much less ski?

'Gently,' she instructed, wanting to wince for him when she saw him gingerly at work with his right boot. 'Let me...' she offered quickly, putting down the boot she held. But then she recalled how on the mountain he had told her she had done more than enough, and held back.

Suddenly, though, she was unable to bear to watch, and looked over the veranda to concentrate her attention on his black Ferrari. Had she really driven that fiery monster?

The 'clonk' of his right boot hitting the wood floor caused her to glance swiftly back at him, her eyes going at once to his sock-clad foot. 'It—doesn't look too swollen,' she commented thoughtfully, although, since he'd probably got several pairs of thick socks on to keep out the cold, it was in truth difficult to tell.

'Should I apologise?' he snarled sarcastically, and Elyn had to wonder at this love business. For while it hurt her that he was hurt, at the same time she felt she could have cheerfully have boxed his ears for his sarcasm. Stormy green eyes looked into his unrepentant dark ones, then, just when she was starting to admit that in all honesty it was her fault that he was in pain—and like a bear with a sore head because of it—he got to his feet, extracted a key from a pocket in his ski-jacket and, opening the door to the chalet, ordered, 'Go and make some coffee.'

'I'll bet they loved you at charm school!' she snapped, and marched into the chalet, hardly crediting that the bark of sound behind her had sounded suspiciously like a bark of laughter. She didn't want to amuse the sarcastic swine—to throttle him would have suited her better!

She walked straight into a sitting-room that was pleasantly furnished with several luxurious rugs over a polished wood floor. There were several doors leading off the sitting-room, but one of them was open and she saw at once that it was a kitchen. She made for it.

The percolator was set to boil when she heard sounds of Max making his way across the sitting-room. Immediately she felt guilty. She should have been there to help him, to let him lean on her.

A door closed somewhere and she knew he had made it to wherever it was without her help. Soon afterwards she heard the sound of running water and realised that, after his skiing exertions, he must be taking a shower. How he was managing to do that when he could barely stand upright without overbalancing was a mystery to her, but knowing a little of the man, she had an idea that if he was decided on something then that would be that. Nothing would stop him.

The coffee had been ready some while when Elyn began to wonder if he'd had his lunch yet. She had a look in the fridge and, espying some bread and cheese, took it out. Then she took off her jacket and got to work. She had just finished making him some cheese sandwiches when she heard him limp into the kitchen behind her. She turned round.

He *had* showered, she saw from his still damp hair, and was now dressed in casual trousers, a shirt and a fine sweater; his feet were bare of shoes and were clad in woollen socks.

'How's the foot?' she asked evenly.

'Strapped up!'

'Good. Where are you having your coffee?'

His answer was to take a chair at the kitchen table. Elyn placed a plate of cheese sandwiches and a cup of coffee in front of him. 'Where's yours?' he asked.

'I had something to eat on the mountain,' she told him.

'Coffee?' he queried, and because it seemed churlish not to, she poured herself a cup. When she turned round again, she could see that he had moved a chair out from the table for her. She took her coffee over and went and sat down.

'I didn't know you were coming here this weekend,' she murmured conversationally.

'Had I known that *you were*, Elyn believe me, I'd have thought twice about it!' he retorted, and suddenly it was her turn to be amused—she couldn't help it. At the barely concealed hint that had he known that out of all the resorts she'd chosen Cavalese and that he'd find her standing there on the ski-run as he came down full pelt, he'd have avoided the place like the plague, her mouth started to curve upwards.

She saw his glance go to her mouth, but suddenly then, as her heartbeats became laboured, her defence mechanism was activated, and she knew she had to guard against him seeing that he could make a nonsense out of her.

'I was coming here with a friend, but he couldn't make it—he had to work,' she added quickly, just in case Max thought that her friend had gone off the idea. 'Anyhow, as the room reservations were made, he suggested I had a lift with his sister, who was coming this way, and...'

'So you're here all alone?' he cut in—and Elyn inwardly groaned. Heaven help her, she must be boring him to tears!

'Yes,' she agreed. 'And you?' she enquired, waving a hand generally about the chalet. 'Are you here on your own?'

He nodded. 'I had this odd notion that I'd like to commune with the elements this weekend.'

Elyn was immediately immensely heartened that there was no madly attractive female on his agenda that weekend, and almost apologised again for being the cause of his accident and spoiling his communion with nature. But, having already thought she must be boring him out of his skull, she thought for a moment, and then, remembering that the Ferrari had been far easier to drive than she had anticipated, she offered, 'I'll drive you back to wherever it is you live, if you like.'

Max was shaking his head long before she finished. 'I'm going nowhere but here until Monday,' he stated determinedly, but relented to enlighten her, 'Because of the hell of a week I've got planned for next week, I've come away this weekend with the express purpose of clearing my brain.'

'You're in Rome next week,' Elyn recalled, and, her sensitivity on the march again, she realised that were he back in his home and laid up with an injured foot, there was every likelihood that he would find some work to do.

'You've remembered,' he commented, and while she thought it unlikely she would forget a word he had ever said to her, she also thought he seemed pleased that she'd remembered that snippet from the time they had shared a meal together.

'Of course,' she said matter-of-factly, but became inwardly agitated in case he recalled how, after that meal, he had taken her home and how, unresisting, she had gone into his arms. 'So you're here until Monday, and I'm returning to Verona on Sunday afternoon,' she added hurriedly, more from a need to say something to get her mind, and his, off such memories than for any other reason.

'How are you getting back?' he enquired mildly.

Elyn gave an inward sigh of relief to feel in safer waters. 'Diletta Agosta, Tino's sister, is picking me up on her way back from visiting her fiancé's family,' she told him, realising only then that she had as good as told him who the friend was she had been coming away with. Not that Max looked devastated by that snippet—she should be so lucky! 'But if you're insisting on staying here, how will you get back?' she asked. If he was taking off from Verona or Bergamo airport for Rome on Monday, he'd still need to somehow get from Cavalese to his own home.

Max shrugged. 'I'll worry about that on Monday,' he drawled, and after a moment or two of looking at her thoughtfully, promptly proceeded to completely astound her, by adding matter-of-factly, 'In the meantime, you can leave your hotel and move in here to look after me.'

'M-move in here?' she exclaimed, staring at him thunderstruck, her heartbeat racing at just that very thought. 'I'm not doing anything of the kind!' she denied her emotions to tell him forthrightly.

'You don't think you owe me something?'

'Not *that* much!' she retorted.

'Even though it's your fault that I can't look after myself?' he challenged, the truth of that weakening her.

'I—er . . .' she mumbled, the weakness of wanting to do nothing better than stay with him, and to look after him joining in the general mêlée of her emotions. 'So,' she found herself agreeing, 'I'll look after you today. But I'll go back to my hotel tonight and come up again in the morning to see if there's anything you need.'

'You're too good to me!' he grunted, and while her heart went out to him, he got up and limped from the kitchen.

Elyn stayed in the kitchen for some while after he had gone. She loved him so much, and the gods were really smiling on her—indeed, must have been working overtime to arrange it—this time alone with him. And yet she felt too shy to move.

She rinsed through the china they had used, then set about generally tidying up the kitchen. She could hear Max moving about in the sitting room, so she knew he hadn't gone to rest his foot up on his bed as she had thought he might.

Once more she investigated the fridge. By the look of it, Max had been intending to have most of his meals out, she concluded. She investigated the cupboards. Macaroni cheese and oven-baked chips from the freezer compartment of the fridge might not do a lot for his gourmet soul, but that was what his stomach was getting for supper!

She checked her watch and was surprised to see that it was gone four o'clock. She was then taken by an overwhelming urge to see him, and left the safety of the kitchen to go to the sitting-room. Max had put a light to a most appealing log fire, she observed, and was now taking his ease on a wooden-armed settee.

'Fancy a cup of tea?' she enquired as he looked over at her, just the sight of him making her heart turn over. She slid her glance from him and to where he had switched on a small table lamp.

'Only if you'll join me,' he accepted pleasantly, and as she glanced back at him Elyn met his gaze full on.

'Right,' she murmured, and got out of there to make it to the kitchen with a fast-beating heart.

'So, tell me about Elyn Talbot,' Max suggested when ten minutes later they sat sharing a pot of tea.

'There's nothing to tell,' she smiled, and, looking from him to his bootless feet, 'Do you mind if I take my boots off too? It's warming up in here.'

'Would you like me to find you a pair of socks?' he enquired.

'Certainly not!' she teased with mock-hauteur. 'I've got my own socks, thank you very much.'

She loved it when he grinned, and swiftly bent down to undo her boots lest he should see from the expression on her face how just to have him good-humoured with her played ducks and drakes with her heart.

'So,' he tried again, 'tell me where Elyn Talbot learned to make such fantastic cheese sandwiches?'

'Oh, Max!' she giggled, and, at the warm look of friendship in his eyes, brought herself up short—this was wonderful, too wonderful; there'd be tears before bedtime. 'At my mother's knee,' she told him soberly, and, feeling all over the place inside, she got to her feet. 'May I investigate the plumbing?' she enquired brightly.

By seven o'clock that evening she knew what lay behind each of the doors in the chalet. At Max's invitation to, 'Take a look round,' she had discovered, by mistakenly opening the bedroom door first, that it was one-bedroomed accommodation, with the most modern of bathrooms being the next-door room. By seven o'clock that evening too she and Max, their talk impersonal, had discussed many things. From the glass that was used in making a mosaic they had moved on to the hard crystalline rock that was used for the sculpture work at Zappelli Internazionale. And from there, admittedly in answer to her many questions, Max had told her a little about Verona, situated as it was at the junction of major routes, and about the many Roman remains to be found there.

She was an avid listener, but when Max again brought the subject around to her with, 'That's enough about my country—tell me, have you always lived in Bovington?' she grew afraid of revealing too much about herself, of perhaps revealing something of her caring—for him—and she could not help but shy away from his questioning.

'If I'm going to get you something to eat for your supper before I return to my hotel, I'd better get a move on,' she declared suddenly, and leapt to her feet.

'Elyn!' Max's stern tone stopped her mid-flight. She paused, and shot him a worried glance.

'Yes?' she asked, and knew she had given away the agitated mess she was inside.

Strangely, though, Max did not—to her great relief—refer to it, but, after several long moments of just looking very solemnly at her, all at once a reassuring half-smile came to his expression. 'I think you should know that I shall refuse to eat a crumb of anything more today—unless you share it with me.'

'Oh,' escaped her.

'Would you see me starve?' he enquired.

'You wait until you see supper!' she warned, and, laughing, 'You might think starving preferable!' With that she headed out into the kitchen, knowing that this man had the power to make a complete nonsense of her.

They had their meal, such as it was, at the kitchen table. 'This is good!' Max complimented her on her efforts with the pasta, cheese and milk.

'I doubt if there's another macaroni cheese quite like it around these parts,' she laughed, caught his gaze on her laughing mouth, and asked brightly, 'How's your foot?'

'I'll survive,' he made light of it.

'You really should rest it, you know,' she told him
seriously.

'You don't think sitting here like this is resting it?'

'You should have it up, or on a level at any rate. It
must be throbbing like the dickens.'

'How do you know such things?' he wanted to know.

'It must be instinctive,' she replied lightly, and because just looking at him was making her emotions go
haywire, she was sorely in need of getting herself under
control. 'Do go and rest,' she urged, 'and I'll bring coffee
into the sitting-room.'

'I'll make it,' he offered.

'That,' she said firmly, 'is not resting.'

'Are all Englishwomen so bossy?' he asked
goodnaturedly.

'They don't get a look-in when it comes to the
bossiness of Italian men,' she retorted cheekily.

'I'll owe you for that,' he threatened, and got up and
limped from the room.

While the coffee was percolating Elyn cleared the table
and washed up. But she felt only marginally less haywire
when she carried a tray of coffee into the sitting-room.
Max was seated on the floor, his back to the settee, his
left leg bent as he looked from the fire and to her.

'There you are, you see, resting,' he teased, pointing
to his stretched-out right leg. 'Come and join me on the
floor,' he invited.

It was as nice a place as any, and in minutes Elyn was
seated on the floor with her back against a solid chair.
Soon she must make tracks back to her hotel, but for
now this was the happiest time of her life, and she did
not want to hurry away from it—not just yet.

The fire was warm, and she toasted her toes in their
white three-quarter-length socks. It was warm in the
sitting-room now and she was glad she had some time
ago removed the sweater she had on over her shirt. She

would be glad of it when she went out—it must be freezing out there.

'So, tell me about Maximilian Zappelli?' she took a leaf out of his book to enquire.

And laughed delightedly when he grinned and said, 'There's too much to tell.'

'I don't doubt it,' she smiled back, and loved him, and looked away lest he saw her love.

But she wasn't sure how she felt when he suggested, 'So, give about, sweet, beautiful Elyn,' and, encouragingly, 'I refuse to believe that there's "nothing to tell".'

'You're a devil for punishment,' she warned, but added, 'Basically, I was born and grew up in Bovington.'

'And worked hard for Sam Pillinger,' he took up. 'But I knew that bit.'

'There isn't any more,' she insisted.

'What about your parents?'

'My parents are divorced,' she said bluntly, an edge she could do nothing about entering her voice. She hoped he would leave it there, but of course he didn't.

'You live with your mother,' he documented.

'And my new family,' she allowed, there being nothing more to say on the subject as far as she was concerned.

'Ever see your father?' he enquired casually.

'Rarely,' Elyn replied, and found she was tacking on, 'Out of sight, out of mind has always been his motto.'

'That upsets you?'

She threw him an impatient look. 'Grief, no!' she scoffed—but her scoffing tone, her impatience, were ignored.

'How old were you when your parents separated?' Max pressed quietly.

For a moment or two she considered not answering, but he was waiting, saying nothing, but just waiting, so she shrugged offhandedly. 'I was twelve when he left us for good,' she saw no harm in telling him, but—and to her staggering amazement—discovered she was confiding, 'But in truth I'm not sure that last time whether he went of his own accord, or if my mother threw him out.'

Feeling shaken that she had said so much, and sorely wanting to blame Max for dragging that out of her, she felt she might have hit him had he dared to make some mocking remark to the effect that her mother must be a weight-lifter to be able to throw her father out.

But Max did not say anything of the kind, and his tone was quiet still, understanding even, when after holding her gaze steadily, speculatively for some long seconds, to her surprise he asked, 'And how did that affect you, Elyn—your parents splitting up?'

Abruptly she looked away from him and into the fire. She made a movement as though to rise, as if to be away. But even while she was trying to remember where she had put her jacket, suddenly he had swiftly slewed round and as if he had read her actions to leave, placed a restraining hand on her arm.

She looked down arrogantly at the hand on her arm as if to show she felt contaminated by his touch. But it had no effect, for his hand stayed firm on her, while he insisted on being answered.

'Does it hurt so much?' he asked.

'Not at all,' she assured him coldly—though again she found her tongue running away from her. 'Divorce was the best thing that could have happened to them.'

'But it scarred you.'

It was a statement, not a question, and at that moment Elyn hated him for his perception. 'If you *must* know, his unfaithfulness to my mother made me loathe that sort of man!' she snapped. 'I saw her hurt by his womanising,' she went on angrily. 'My father made her unhappy on too many occasions...'

'And that made you unhappy too?'

Elyn threw him a withering look. She didn't want this conversation. 'Some!' she muttered. But then, to her absolute horror, words were coming to her, were queueing up, pouring from her—and she didn't seem able to do a thing to stop them! Short, angry words fell from her lips as she snapped, 'There were rows—my stars, there were rows! Crockery flying! Violent words, actions! He was always off with some woman, always in debt—and so were we! There was never any money...' Her voice started to go wobbly, began to trail off. She wanted to stop, but somehow, having got started, she didn't seem able to! 'I grew up h-hating debt, and vowing that I would n-never owe any—any...' Her voice fractured, and all at once Max took her gently in his arms.

'Let it all out, *cara*,' he breathed soothingly. 'You've held it in for far too long.'

A shuddery kind of sob went through her, and Elyn felt swamped by a hail of differing emotions as she murmured shakily, 'I don't think there's any more to let out.'

'There were perhaps years of pent-up emotion in you waiting to be released,' Max suggested, and all she could do was smile a quavery smile.

'So when did you graduate from psychology college?' she asked, no longer angry with him—only in love.

'Brave little one,' he murmured, his answering smile warm and making her feel so good that when he bent his head as though to salute her bravery, she turned her face to his, and invited his kiss.

'Oh, Max,' she whispered shakenly, and he smiled down into her upturned face, then gently kissed her again.

Only this time her arms went up and around him, and it was so good to hold him close and, as she felt his arms tighten about her, to be held close by him.

The next time he kissed her there was a subtle change in his kiss. His mouth was gentle still, but firmer, gently seeking. Oh, Max, Max! she wanted to cry, but he had her lips held captive, so she just held him more fiercely to her.

Then all at once there was passion in his firm kisses, and Elyn wanted more. She felt his hands at her back roving over her thin shirt, and then her shirt was separated from the waistband of her trousers.

'Beautiful Elyn,' he murmured against her mouth, and as a groan of wanting left her, she felt his warm wonderful hands on the bare skin of her waist.

'Max!' she moaned his name aloud, her hands caressing upwards to his thick dark hair, only to fall, and grip hard on to his shoulders when his hands beneath her shirt caressed upwards until at last her breasts were held captive.

She wanted to cry his name again, but couldn't. She was afraid when tenderly he undid the clasp of her bra, his hands now capturing the naked skin of the swelling globes, but she was afraid, not of him, but that her tongue might betray her, and end it all. She had said 'no' before from the shock of his touch. She pressed herself to him, in a mindless arousal of wanting. If she said a word at all, she wanted that word to be 'yes.'

His lips were still pressed to hers as he undid her shirt and slipped it off her. Her bra disappeared with it, and though she felt a moment's shyness, she bravely overcame it. When Max divested himself of his shirt and sweater and she felt the warm and wonderful touch of his hair-roughened skin against the satin-smoothness of her own body, Elyn luxuriated in the touch.

His long sensitive fingers circled the hardened tips of her breasts, and a groan of wanting escaped her. But shyness smote her again when a few minutes later his gentle fingers ceased doing mind-bending things to the hard pink peaks he had created and he pulled back to look at her. With the soft light of the table lamp behind him, his glance rested on her beautiful breasts, the glow and shadow of the firelight enhancing their beauty.

'Oh, *cara*, my dear!' he breathed, and while Elyn hoped he would think the warm colour in her cheeks

came solely from the fire and not from the shyness of
a man seeing her uncovered form for the first time, he
leaned forward and kissed first one breast and then the
other.

'Max!' She clutched at him and just had to cry his
name. She wanted him, wanted him! His kisses, the moist
inside of his mouth as his lips and tongue caressed and
moulded one breast while enticing fingers gently moulded
the other, were sending her into a frenzy of wanting.

She clutched him again, and pressed closer still to him,
loving the freedom she had to touch his skin. She adored
him, and adored what he was doing to her when tenderly, the warm rug beneath them, he moved her to lie
down.

Somehow they were both divested of all but the
minimum of clothing, and his body was so close it was
like a second skin against hers when, their bare legs
mingling, he came to lie over her.

'Oh, Max!' she cried. And when the fire in her body
for him became too much to contain, 'Oh, please,
please,' she urged, 'take me!'

'My dear!' he cried exultantly, and kissed her, his
hands at the band of her briefs.

Soon she knew she would be without a stitch of
clothing. It was what she wanted and, in a mindless un-
thinking world of her need for him, her love, she just
had to tell him, 'I want you. I've never wanted a man
before. But now—now I know that consuming need,
know what that need feels like—oh, Max, please,' she
begged feverishly, 'I've never...' The strangled sound
that left him, the hoarse cry of something in his own
language when, as though suddenly scalded, his hand
left her briefs, caused her to break off, startled.

She was more utterly dumbfounded than startled,
though, when his next action was to roll hurriedly away
from her, to put some space between them and to sit up

and present her with his wide-shouldered, broad, won-derful naked back!

'Max... What...?' she asked helplessly, desperately trying to find some sense in what was happening now. Max had been about to claim her, to make her his, to take her to new passions, to ease this aching undeniable need he had created in her, so what was he doing, sitting over there? 'Oh!' she exclaimed as a small part of her brain started to function. 'Oh, Max, I'm sorry—your foot! Did I...'

'Forget it!' he snarled, and if he'd thrown a bucket of cold water over her, his tone couldn't have had a better effect. Clearly, he had gone off wanting to make love to her.

'*Forget* it?' she exclaimed before she could help it. But pride, even then ever a fierce ally, was there to help her out. My stars, she would not beg! Though she was still confused as she stammered proudly, 'Con-consider it done!' and in that moment of overwhelming rejection she hoped his foot was hurting him like hell. Agitatedly she spotted her boots by the fireplace, but there was no way she was going near him again. Nor—when only a minute before she had given him every freedom with her naked body—was he going to catch so much as a glimpse of a bare arm. 'If you'll pass my b-boots back, please,' she requested chokily, 'I'll get to my hotel.'

She was already fastening up her bra and reaching for her shirt when he informed her harshly, 'You're going nowhere, the state you're in!' and while Elyn began to hate him because he was so familiar with women that he knew the state she was in, knew the havoc he had created on her senses, he decreed, 'You can have the bedroom, I'll sleep out here.'

Like hell, she thought, but then realised two things. One that, since Max had gone completely off the idea of making love to her, she would not have an unwelcome visitor during the night, the other—as she looked at the

wooden arms of the settee—that anyone who slept on
that was in for the most appalling night!

He deserved worse, but that would do for a start.
'Thanks, I will!' she accepted snappily and, snatching
up the rest of her clothes as she went, she stormed out
of the sitting-room into the one and only bedroom. But
she knew, the moment she had closed the door on him,
that Max wasn't the one who was in for a most appalling night!

CHAPTER SEVEN

THE night seemed endless, and Elyn was never more glad to see dawn tiptoe across the sky. Her head ached from a combination of lack of sleep and the torture of thought after thought that had gone through her head, over and over, during those wakeful hours.

Initially she had been too emotionally overwrought to think very clearly at all. But gradually her emotions had become a shade more even, and she was then afflicted by an unanswerable why, why, why?

Why had Max stopped making love to her? Why? So abruptly? So...how could he? She had been lost to everything, so how could he stop!

Somehow she felt she could discount the possibility that his injured foot had had anything to do with it. There had been not an atom of pain in his tone when, in answer to her comment about his foot, he'd hurled that snarled 'Forget it!' at her.

So, with passion soaring, leading the way, taking charge of her—and him, she had thought—if Max had been anywhere near as unconscious of anything save their two selves, the way she had been, then there was no way he would have so suddenly rolled away from her the way that he had.

Which, she realised on the third time round of that question, answered that part of it. Quite clearly Max had not been anywhere near as unconscious as she had been.

But what had put him off? Had she been too gauche? Too eager? Her face flamed at the thought. She hadn't put up so much as a minimum amount of resistance, had she? Was that it? Had she been to easy a conquest?

Oh, heavens, she cringed in shame, men like Max liked a challenge. He wouldn't be where he was today in business if he did not care for the cut and thrust of challenge in his business life. But, on the personal side of it—she, with her 'please, please take me,' had represented no challenge whatsoever! Her face flamed afresh as she recalled how she had *begged* him to take her. Oh, lord, how would she ever be able to face him again?

Desperately she tried to find release from her mortification by remembering that he still wasn't convinced that she was not some design thief. But in her heart of hearts she felt it had nothing to do with that. Max hadn't been thinking business when she'd been warm and willing in his arms. He had wanted her, she knew that, she wasn't so naïve that she had misunderstood *that*! At one point, he had been as eager as she—until she had begged him to take her.

Elyn's face started to grow scarlet again, and, knowing that all she wanted to do was to get out of there, she went and listened at the bedroom door. She could hear not a sound and realised that, against all odds, there was a fair chance he was sound asleep on that hard-armed settee.

She was aware that she couldn't return to her hotel in the state she was in, and since the bathroom was only next door, she decided to slip out—no need to so much as glance at the settee—and nip into the bathroom to freshen up.

Part one of her plan worked, and she stared at herself in the bathroom mirror, but could see no sign of her inner torment. Stripping off her clothes, she rinsed her briefs through, dried them in a towel and put them on the radiator to finish off drying while she had a bath.

She was towelling herself dry, though, when, as she was going over again what had led up to Max taking her in his arms in the first place, it suddenly struck her that the reason she had not wanted him to ask questions about her parents—her father in particular—was that she had been feeling happy and did not want to be reminded of her father. Because, in doing so, as well as dragging up old hurts, she would be reminded that, like her father, Max too was a philanderer.

Elyn was dressed, save for her boots which were still in the sitting-room, and was combing her long blonde hair when suddenly her comb stilled. For, while she was recalling the passion of Max's lovemaking, suddenly, like a bolt from the blue, she found she was wondering, was Max such a philanderer after all? Having ruled out the notion that his injured foot had anything to do with it, would a philanderer who was within an ace of achieving his goal—to score another bed victory—call a halt when that victory was his for the taking? It was true he was often seen dating the most glamorous of women, but wasn't he free and unattached? And, loath though she was to defend him, he was a most eligible bachelor, and as such, since he worked so hard, was it a sin not to stay home nights?

Suddenly Elyn knew that, unlike her father, who would probably bed where he could, Max had more finesse than that, and suddenly she realised that Max was very choosy. She had no need to look further than last night to see that if it did not seem right to him, then right there, at the eleventh hour, so to speak, Max had sufficient control to call a halt.

All of which left her feeling in no way less bruised when, with nothing to return to the bedroom for, she left the bathroom—and looked towards the settee! With relief she saw that Max was not there, was not even in the sitting-room. Good, she thought, her turbulent insides becoming marginally more calm, and she went over to collect her snow-boots and sat down to put them on.

Damn him! she fumed, when she found she was wondering where he was and if he could walk on that foot
this morning. As if she cared! She'd have heard him if
he'd gone out, she knew that, so she was sure he was in
the kitchen—which was another piece of rotten luck, because the kitchen was where her jacket was!

For several minutes Elyn sat where she was and con-
templated leaving minus her jacket. When common sense
bombarded her, however, and insisted that, without the
freezing cold out there, she was being plain ridiculous,
she impatiently got to her feet and went into the kitchen.

He was there. As she had surmised, Max was there in
the kitchen. Clean-shaven to denote that she had not
been the first visitor to the bathroom that morning, he
was sitting, feet under the table, facing the door as she
went in. Colour flared to her face, but she ignored him—
it annoyed her that he ignored her too.

She went past him and retrieved her jacket, and with
nothing more to hang around for, without even pausing
to put it on, she went, head in the air, sailing back past
him again.

She had almost made it to the door when, his tone
not the pleasantest she had ever heard, he stopped her.
'You can't leave!' he grated.

Watch me, she wanted to throw over her shoulder, but
her heart, stupid as it was where he was concerned, made
her turn round. Oh, lord, how dear he was to her! 'Why
not?' she asked belligerently, that tone greatly at odds
with the way she was feeling inside.

She watched as his black-as-thunder expression roved
her unmade-up face, and was glad of her creamy flawless
complexion. 'You think it fair,' he rapped, 'that you
should injure me—and then waltz off without giving a
thought to how I will manage?'

What about me? she wanted to hurl at him. What
about my injuries, my hurt? You don't give a damn about
how *I* will manage! Hostilely she glared at him, and hos-

tilely he glared back. Get lost, fumed her head. 'So what do you want for breakfast?' she shot at him unpleasantly as her ridiculous heart, as she knew it would, let her down on account of the pain he must be in.

'You've used up all the cheese!' he accused.

'So?' she snapped.

'So there's a tin of sardines—we'll have those on toast.'

Thinking of telling him he could have the whole tin to himself, Elyn draped her jacket over a chair and got to work. She was aware, though, of his antagonistic glance following her as she deftly made coffee and sardines on toast. She was about to pile her efforts all on to one plate, however, when suddenly rebellion set in and she went and found another plate. Why should he have all the sardines? She was doing all the work!

Mainly because she thought it would be childish in the extreme to take her plate into the sitting-room, Elyn sat down at the table to eat her breakfast. It was a silent meal. She had nothing she wanted to say to him, and that, it seemed, went double for him.

The small repast over, she collected their used dishes and took them to the sink. She'd cut her tongue out before she'd ask how his injured foot was this morning, she fumed, though she guessed it must be giving him some trouble or, proud man that he was, he would never have intimated that he could not manage without some help.

'Now what?' she demanded, when, everything spick and span and his 'you can't leave' rattling around in her head, she baulked at the idea of sitting staring at him in stony silence for the rest of the morning.

It didn't take two guesses to realise that he must have been thinking the self-same thing, because he ordered, 'You can take me out for a drive!'

Yesterday she'd have had heart failure at the thought. Today was a different matter. 'I trust you'll be able to make it to the car without my shoulder,' she returned pithily, just to let him know that she'd hit him if he so much as laid a finger on her that morning—prop or no prop.

Hardening her heart, she left Max to hobble about finding some shoes from his weekend bag in the bedroom, while she went to the sitting-room to set about clearing out the ashes from yesterday's fire. She was in the process of generally making the place presentable for their return when he limped past her to the outside door.

Thinking to give him time to get into the Ferrari, she spent another few minutes straightening cushions and furniture, then went and donned her jacket.

She saw from the veranda that he was comfortably ensconced in the Ferrari, and she was just about to join him when she noticed that the ski-boots he'd taken off yesterday were still where he left them. They were as heavy today as yesterday, she mused as she transferred them from the cold outside air and popped them round the door to just inside the sitting-room to thaw out. Max had put the key in the outer door, she noticed. She turned it, and went to join him.

'Key!' she said briefly, passing it over to him as she got into the driver's seat of the Ferrari.

'Thanks,' he returned shortly and, the ignition key already in place, Elyn started up the engine. It was the sum total of any conversation for quite some while.

Not that she wanted to talk, for as they went upwards and into snowy terrain, as they drove around hairpin bends, with the occasional sheer drop on the driver's side, she had to keep all her attention on her driving.

The sun was shining, and as Max instructed her to park the car in a place called Oclini, she was content just to sit there and gaze at the fir trees and the progress of the Sunday skiers. There did not seem to be anywhere as near as many people at Oclini as there had been skiing on Alpe Cermis yesterday, Elyn considered. Though since

Alpe Cermis was where Max had, through her, met with his accident, she did not want to think about it.

Some contrary monster within her, however, was loosening her tongue, and even though she had determined that his foot could drop off before she would enquire after it, she heard her treacherous other self enquire, 'How's the foot?'

'How do you think?' he grunted, and she could as easily given him a black eye to go with it.

'How long do you want to stay here?' she asked—that or hit him!

'Bored already?' he jibed.

'It's the company I keep!' she snapped, and for one infinitesimal moment she thought she saw the corners of his mouth twitch—as if he found her spirited rejoinder amusing.

'You can drive back down to Lavaze,' he instructed, not a smile in sight. 'We'll have coffee there.'

Without a word Elyn started up the car and steered it back down the way they had come, taking her time because of oncoming traffic and sharp bends. But ten minutes later Max was telling her to drop him off at a hotel and restaurant and instructing her where to park. 'If you're ordering, I'll have tea,' she told him, just to be perverse, as he got out of the car and stood waiting for her to drive off.

It did not take long to park the car, but even so there was a glass of tea there waiting for her when she joined him on the sun veranda. She turned her chair into the sun, donned her sunglasses and listened to the silence broken only by the occasional sound of some skier or cross-country ski-walker briefly in their vicinity. They seemed to have the veranda to themselves.

'Thanks,' she tossed in Max's general direction as she took her first sip of tea. It was a glorious day and, given that he was a swine, good manners cost nothing.

There was a silence for about five minutes, then, as
if he too was doing his best to resurrect his manners,
Max drawled casually, 'You're a good driver.'

She gave him a sideways glance, but he had sunglasses
on too, and she could read nothing from his expression.
But, while it did her heart good that his distant arctic
tone had gone, she still wasn't in a mood to turn cart-
wheels for him. 'One does one's best,' she shrugged—
though she had to admit that her own tone was a shade
or two warmer.

'What make of car do you drive in England?' he asked,
his tone almost conversational.

'I don't. I sold it,' she answered, without thinking,
and was annoyed in the next second that this man seemed
to constantly get under her guard, seemed to constantly
have her confiding matters which she had no intention
of confiding. She sent him an irritated look.

Had she hoped that by doing so, however, he would
realise he had trespassed, albeit accidentally, on private
ground and would change the subject, she realised she
should have known better. 'You sold it?' he questioned—she decided not to answer. 'Why?' he wanted
to know, and ignoring the fact that she was not hiding
her feelings of exasperation with him he commented,
'Not in exchange for another one, or you'd have a car
now.' You're so clever, you work it out, she fumed
silently—and could have hit him when he did. Because
'Ah!' he uttered after a few silent seconds, and, ever
ready with his questions, 'I hadn't realised that things
were *that* bad!'

'What do you mean, *that* bad?' she flared hostilely.

He ignored her hostility. 'I heard that Pillingers only
just managed to fight off bankruptcy,' he explained, 'but
I'd no idea that you each had to sell off your private
vehicle to achieve it.'

'I was the only one to sell!' Elyn retorted hotly. 'We...'

'You were the only one?' he interrupted, facing her now and appearing to be trying to pierce the darkness of her sunglasses with his gaze.

'We didn't have to sell *anything*!' she snapped proudly, as she would have done had he given her time to finish. 'For your information, we...'

'Then why sell your car if...' Abruptly he halted, and then, his voice suddenly gentle, 'Oh, Elyn!' he murmured softly. 'You were so terrified of debt that you...'

But Elyn was finding his switch to a gentle, understanding tone crucifying. 'Huh!' she scorned. 'We're not paupers yet, you know!'

'Maybe not,' he agreed, 'but it's my guess that you panicked at the thought of no money coming in, at the thought of outstanding debt, and sold your car.' Elyn refused to answer—but that didn't stop him. 'So,' he proceeded, 'even after you'd sold your car, your hang-up over debt still tortured you, and you looked around for work to ensure an income.'

'I'd have worked anyway, found myself a job!' she retorted loftily. 'The fact that your Pinwich subsidiary happened to advertise work I could do, and happened to be paying the best salary around, was something I had to take when I applied.'

He didn't like her lofty tone, she could tell that from the sudden aggressive thrust of his chin. But, when she had thought that she had at last succeeded in getting him to drop the subject, she discovered that she had done nothing of the sort. And what was more, that he had looked beneath her last statement and wasn't above tackling her about that either.

A certain coolness entered his tone. 'You sound as if you had to swallow great quantities of that mammoth Talbot pride before you could bring yourself to apply for work at my Pinwich operation?' he challenged. 'You sound as though you blame me in some way?' he grated.

And pushed into a corner, perhaps of her own making, her back rigid as she faced him, Elyn used some of that mammoth pride to get herself out. 'Is it any wonder?' she questioned arrogantly. 'Is it any wonder that I had to swallow my pride—that my family was appalled when I told them that I was going to work for the opposition, and that...'

'Opposition!'

Elyn ignored the fact that he seemed surprised. 'The firm that had a major hand in Pillingers' folding!' she snapped angrily.

Though if she was hostile, then Max was doubly so, and was letting her get away with nothing when he rapped bluntly, 'Do not talk rubbish!'

'*Rubbish*?' she flared.

'The only people responsible for Pillingers' downfall are Pillinger himself and market forces.'

'Market forces don't seem to have affected you that much!' she accused, and, seething because he was blaming her dear stepfather, 'And we were doing all right before you came on the scene and stole our best workers!'

'Stole them!' he echoed furiously. 'As you've re-marked yourself, I pay good wages...'

'Implying that since we paid peanuts we got left with the monkeys!' she erupted. 'Well, let me tell you, Signor Zappelli, we trained those people...'

'And got your money's worth out of them before they came to us!' he clipped. 'If you didn't have the foresight to pin them down by a contract...'

'We relied on loyalty!'

'Then more fool you! The first principle of...'

But Elyn wasn't listening. Utterly furious with him, she sprang up from her chair and stormed away. The vile pig! How dared he! Smart swine, with his sharp tongue and up-to-the-minute business methods!

Having stormed away from him, Elyn had no in-tention of going back to the car, so she made for the road in an opposite direction and walked along fuming. She should have stayed to argue it out with him, she seethed but she had felt so incensed by his arrogant attitude—she ignored the fact that her arrogance had been a fairly good match to his—that she had come near to hitting him.

A stitch in her side caused her to slow her pace a little, and she slowed some more to stop and watch a few people on the cross-country ski-walk—*langlauf*, she thought it was called—and gradually she began to grow calmer.

Only then was she able to accept that it wasn't Max who was a vile pig, but the pig of it was being in love. Normally, she knew, she would have stayed to finish off any argument, but being in love had made her too emotional, too emotional to think rationally.

She turned round and slowly began to retrace her steps, doing some very rational thinking as she went. The sum total of which brought her the plain and honest truth that Max was a better businessman than Sam. She had worked in both companies and knew, if she were starting up her own company, which model she would follow.

It was no use blaming anyone but themselves, she realised that now. And she even accepted then, as she made her way back to the car, that some of the blame for Pillingers' demise lay at her door. She should *somehow* have made Sam listen to her when she had tried to tell him how bad things were. True, nobody could have foreseen that Hutton's were going to call in the receiver, and collapse owing them money. But in no way could Max be held responsible for that.

He was standing by the Ferrari. Elyn saw him glance her way as she approached, and belatedly realised that she still had the car keys, so he could not get in. Oh, grief, she thought, when on coming closer she saw the grimness of his expression. Clearly he was still as mad as hell with her, at her unveiled hint that he had made

Pillingers fold. Elyn thanked her lucky stars then that she still had the keys to the car, otherwise she had a fairly shrewd idea that, injured foot or no injured foot, he would have got into the car and driven off and abandoned her.

It was then, though, that realising that with a foot that must be throbbing like hell he was standing there waiting for her, contritely she speeded up her pace. Poor love, he must be in agony, and here she was . . .

It was then that she realised her emotions were in such an uproar again that she felt much too vulnerable to say a word. She unlocked the car and got in and fiddled about with the ignition, while Max, having settled himself comfortably, closed the passenger door. 'Where to now?' she enquired evenly, politely.

Without so much as a glance her way, Max consulted his watch. 'We'll go down as far as Varena and stop there for some lunch,' he decided.

Elyn was not in the least hungry. Love, she supposed, fighting with Max, had done that to her. But since there was nothing very much to eat back at the chalet, and since he wasn't leaving until tomorrow—and it was starting to worry her how with that sore foot he was going to make it back to his home, let alone Rome— then he was going to need something more than the breakfast sardines on toast he'd eaten to sustain him.

Without another word she set the car in motion and drove steadily down the twists and turns until they reached Varena. 'We'll eat here,' he told her curtly, pointing to a hotel, and, his short tone getting to her, she parked the car and got out.

'I'll leave you to lock up,' she said on seeing that the hotel, built as it was on the mountainside, had a long flight of steps up to the entrance. She handed him the car keys, hoping he'd think she was going to find the ladies' room, when in actual fact, with her emotions all out of gear, she couldn't bear to watch him limp heavily and painfully up all those stairs.

She left him knowing that she would soon get shot down in flames by him should she dare to suggest that they lunched somewhere more on the flat. The way she was feeling just then, she couldn't face another row—not without bursting into tears.

In the ladies' room she gave herself the sternest talking to. When was the last time she had ever burst into tears, for goodness' sake! Though when she left her sanctuary and walked up to him, she knew it had been one thing back there to tell herself to buck her ideas up, and quite another when she saw him again.

'I thought, as it's such a sunny day, that you might like to eat outside,' Max stated coolly.

'Fine,' she agreed, and, seeing a glass door that led to some chairs and tables at the back of the hotel, she went outside.

At any other time she knew she would have adored the peacefulness of the scene. But she was not feeling at peace within herself, and far less so when Max limped out to join her.

Conversation between them was limited to 'please' and 'thank you' in relation to salt or Parmesan cheese, and for Elyn it was the worst mealtime she had ever known. She wanted to be away from Max, and at the same time, not knowing when she would ever see him again, she did not want to be away from him.

She concentrated her attention on a clutch of hens on the mountainside above who were scratching about, and was never more ready than when Max clipped, 'Shall we go?'

Her answer was to hold out her hand for the car keys. Their hands touched as he passed his keys over, and as a tingle of electricity shot up her arm, it was all she could do not to snatch her hand away.

She left him and was behind the steering wheel of the car when he joined her some minutes later. This time, though, she did not ask him, 'Where to now?' but started up the Ferrari and drove back down to the chalet. When Max made no objection as she parked the car on the drive, she knew that, while she was feeling out of sorts, he'd had enough too.

'I won't come in,' she told him stiffly, as he got out of the car, and she followed suit.

His answer was to nod and, not giving her a chance to thank him, he turned away from her. Abruptly Elyn turned away from him, and bit her lip. Damn him, she loved him! She set off down the hill. What did she want to thank him for anyway? Her lunch? She couldn't even remember what she'd eaten!

She was halfway between the chalet and the outskirts of Cavalese town when she slowed to a halt. Dammit—it was no good! Max hadn't got any food in. He couldn't even drive! And how in creation was he going to get to an airport to fly to Rome tomorrow!

Reluctantly she turned round and set off back up the hill. She knew then that she was acting on emotion, but for heaven's sake, she wouldn't leave someone whom she didn't love to fend for themselves if they were injured, so how on earth could she leave someone whom she did love to do so?

With the idea of perhaps driving to some shops for provisions or, if he was agreeable, driving Max to book into a hotel where she could be certain he'd have room service if nothing else, Elyn made it to the veranda and tested the door into the chalet.

It yielded to her touch. She slipped her sunglasses into her jacket pocket, and went in. Rehearsing some tactful suggestion as she went, she began to cross the sitting-room floor, while at the same time Max, who must have heard someone coming in, came out of the kitchen to investigate. Elyn stopped dead, her eyes widening as Max took another three, maybe four steps nearer. Then, at the sudden and utterly floored expression on her face, so too did he stop dead.

Though it was he who found his voice first. 'Elyn, I...' he began, but Elyn, her emotions already out of gear, was not ready to listen to a word.

'You're not limping!' she gasped, struggling for comprehension. She was still trying to come to terms with that when it sank in that since he *had* been limping half an hour ago, he must have undergone a dramatic healing. 'You didn't hurt yourself at all!' she exclaimed incredulously. And suddenly all hell broke loose in her. 'Why, you...!' she yelled, and as her already haywire emotions jangled completely out of control, her temper went into orbit. Knowing only that she had been well and truly conned, she could only act on a furious anger that demanded to be released, and in a flash she had stormed forward, her hand arcing through the air. 'Take that and try it out on the ski-slopes!' she erupted and, beside herself with rage, she caught him a vicious and unrepentant blow on the side of his face.

She was already on her way when he croaked, 'Elyn!' in shaken tones. Then, 'Elyn, wait!' he called, clearly getting over his astonishment that she had actually hit him. But she was waiting for nothing. Fury such as she had never known was in charge of her; she had only one aim in mind, and that was to get out of there.

At the door, though, she had to pause briefly to open it. That was when she half turned and, as she had the door open, saw that he was coming after her. Unlike her mother, Elyn had never in her life thrown anything in temper. But having, so to speak, just thrown her best punch, she had never been infuriated or hurt past enduring before either, and as the full import of Max's treachery slammed into her, she reached for the nearest missile.

As if it weighed nothing she picked up the solid ski-boot that was there by the door and, as he advanced towards her, she picked it up in that instant and with all her might hurled it at him.

'Elyn!' he yelled her name, but she wasn't listening.

Save for hearing the dreadful clatter and thud as the boot landed, she was out of there on her way, hoping she'd crippled the swine. Because he had crippled her. For clearly he had only pretended injury from some plan to get her to stay with him overnight. Clearly, from that very moment of coming off his skis on that mountainside, he had thought to seduce her. But, equally clearly, she had come on much too strong, had responded much too eagerly, and had put him off the whole idea.

The swine, that he should go to such elaborate lengths—and then reject her! She felt then that she would never, ever recover from the humiliation of it! Oh, how she wished she'd stayed another second or two, just long enough to throw the other heavy ski-boot at him!

CHAPTER EIGHT

ELYN was still feeling bruised and shaken when she showered and dressed and got ready for work the next morning. She had no memory at all of how she got back to her hotel in Cavalese, though she could remember getting her belongings together and sitting in her room waiting for Diletta Agosta to call for her on her way home.

Diletta had been late in picking her up, and by the time she had arrived Elyn had been through a whole welter of emotions. Her anger gone—that was to say, she was able to conceal it and even find a smile to reply, 'That's quite all right. Did you enjoy your weekend?' in answer to Diletta's profuse apologies for being late.

Somehow, too, Elyn managed to suppress her emotions all through the drive back to Verona. But by the time Diletta dropped her off at her apartment, her emotions were fracturing around the edges.

It did not surprise her that she had a horrendous night. She barely slept, and was up early, still feeling hurt and humiliated—Max, despite his 'Elyn, wait!' couldn't even be bothered to follow her, which just showed how much he cared! She had seen for herself when he'd come strolling—limp-free—out of the kitchen that there was nothing whatsoever the matter with his right foot—so, despite her own speed, he could have easily caught up with her, if he'd had a mind to.

But that was just it—he neither cared nor had a mind to so much as apologise for playing some trick on her for his own amusement. How could he, how *could* he? she fumed yet again, once more feeling churned up inside

about what she should do now. Go home, return to
England, her pride decreed, and she had her case half
packed when her old fear of debt jumped on her back.
If she walked out now, she would be walking out of a
well-paid job—and pride wasn't going to put money into
the family coffers, was it?

Against that, though, would Max want to continue to
employ her? She doubted if it was every day that one
of his employees served him the blow she had served
him and remained on the payroll. Though, whatever else
he wasn't, she somehow knew that he was fair. Had he
not been fair he would have dismissed her out of hand
when, all evidence pointing to her as the culprit, that
design had gone missing. So, although he had played her
for a fine fool that weekend, surely he must see that, in
all fairness, he had had that slap coming!

Elyn was still feeling agitated when she made her way
to the computer section of Zappelli Internazionale. That
she'd got this far, she realised, meant that her head was
ruling her heart and that she was not walking out of her
job. Though when Tino Agosta beamed, 'Good morning,
Elyn,' and after enquiring about her own weekend went
on to enthuse about his computer weekend, she began
to think differently. Quite plainly Tino's head was still
full of everything he'd heard and learned and more im-
portantly, he was, she just knew, itching to put some of
it into practice. She, she recognised without hurt or of-
fence, was slowing him up and must be getting in the
way of what he wanted to be doing.

'I rather wanted a word with Felicita Rocca,' she told
Tino when at around half-past nine she could not fault
the idea growing in her head. Indeed, it seemed the only
way. 'Do you have her extension number?'

'Of course,' he said and, his mind so full of things
'computerish', he did not enquire why she should want
to speak to his employer's PA, but picked up the inside

phone and dialled her number, then handed the phone
to Elyn.

From Elyn's point of view it seemed heaven-sent that
Max was in Rome all this week. Though since it was
Felicita Rocca who had done all the arranging for her
to come to Italy, it must be Felicita who, in his absence,
she must see about arranging a transfer back to
England—before the week was out, preferably.

'Hello, it's Elyn Talbot,' she said as she heard Felicita
on the other end of the phone, and, hoping that with
her boss away Felicita wouldn't be so frantically busy,
'May I pop along and see you some time?' she enquired.

'You have a problem, Elyn?' Felicita sounded
concerned.

'Nothing urgent,' Elyn lied. 'But if I could see you
some time this morning.'

She put down the phone having arranged to see Felicita
at eleven, and spent the next hour in sorting out the best
and most tactful way of saying that she wanted to go
back home, quickly—like, yesterday.

At ten to eleven she left her office and walked through
the corridors of the building. She was five minutes early,
but returning to England with all speed had now become
her number one priority. She knocked at Felicita's door
and went in.

'Elyn!' Felicita greeted her charmingly, and leaving
her desk, 'Come in and take a chair and tell me how I
may help you.'

Elyn waited until they were both seated, then, there
being no way to dress it up, she discovered, 'Actually,'
she began, 'I was wondering about the possibility of a
transfer back to England. I would have asked Mr...'
But her lie about how she would have asked Mr Zappelli
had he been there was not needed, she found to her relief.

'You want to leave us?' Felicita exclaimed in surprise.

'If it could be arranged,' Elyn smiled, striving in the
face of Felicita's regret not to feel guilty.

'But I do not think Signor Zappelli would wish you to return so soon,' Felicita put up the first objection.

'Oh, I'm sure he won't mind,' Elyn proceeded to knock it down. 'It's not as if I'm frantically busy here, and I feel a lot of my skills are going to waste. Skills,' she stressed, 'which I could be fully utilising back at our English branch.'

'Mmm—I do not know,' Felicita murmured. But then, while Elyn was starting to blush at the idea that maybe Felicita knew there was something of a cloud hanging over her head in the shape of that missing design, and might be trying to think up some tactful way of telling her that there was not a chance of her returning to England until their employer said so, Felicita went on to say something that took all such thoughts out of Elyn's head. 'It is a decision I cannot make, Elyn,' she explained, and rocked her to her foundations when she trotted out smilingly, 'But I promise I will discuss it with the *signor* when I see him later today.'

'He's coming *here*!' Elyn exclaimed, and, too startled to care if Felicita should wonder that she was privy to his work itinerary. 'He's not in Rome?'

'Unfortunately for him, no,' Felicita replied solemnly. 'Apparently, some time over the weekend, I believe, he twisted his ankle.' Elyn's eyes were growing wider and wider in disbelief when Felicita added, 'He is now at his home and is unable to put his foot to the floor.' This is where I came in! Elyn fumed silently. 'So now he has requested that I drive to his home with some substitute papers. I shall be leaving in a few minutes.' And I made *excuses* for the philandering swine! Elyn thought, outraged, as Felicita ended, 'But naturally, I will mention your request to return to England when...'

'It doesn't matter,' Elyn butted in, her insides churning with jealousy. She had never thought of Max as having an affair with his PA, but... 'It's not so urgent that I'd want you to bother him on his sick bed,' she went on, but as the word 'bed' turned a knife in her, she got up and walked to the door. 'I'll leave it until he's on his feet again.' She even found a smile, and got out of there, her emotions in uproar, but her pride intact—just.

The diabolical rat! she raged, when in the ladies' cloakroom she fought to pull herself together. Substitute papers? Substitute bed-partner, more like! Twisted ankle? Ye gods!

No doubt he found the idea of being incapacitated so that some female had to stay overnight too good not to use a second time. But Felicita? So much for him saying that he never dated anybody from within the company! Though, on thinking about it, he had no need to *date* at all, did he? His PA was going to his home!

There was no denying that Felicita was an attractive woman, but... Elyn had felt hurt before, but as raw jealousy mingled with that hurt, she was again discounting that Max was no philanderer. He damn well was—and the only reason she had tried to believe that he wasn't was that she hadn't been able to accept that, when she had been his for the taking, he had turned her down!

Elyn reeled from the ladies' room back to the computer-room. She'd had it! The fact that Max was having a fling with his PA, and probably had been even while he had been kissing her, was more than she could take. Her fear of debt was in no way diminished—but there were some instances in life, she was discovering, when one's fears had to take second place. Damn the money, damn the job—she was leaving!

'You are all right, Elyn?' Tino asked in concern when she went into the computer-room to pick up her bag and jacket. 'You are very pale in the face!'

Pale in the face? She was flaming—with anger—inside! 'I've got a thundering headache,' she lied, as good manners came to her aid and decreed that no one should be made to feel uncomfortable by her yelling that she was leaving. 'I think I'll go home and lie down for a while.'

'I will drive you,' Tino offered promptly, and was halfway off his chair when Elyn stopped him.

'I prefer to walk, Tino, thank you,' she smiled. 'I think a walk in the fresh air may help my head.'

He looked about to argue, but just then one of the others in the room said something to him in Italian, and Elyn reached for her bag just as Tino passed the message on, 'There is a telephone call for you, Elyn.'

'For me?' she questioned, instantly thinking that Felicita might be ringing her, but just then observing that the phone that was being held out for her was not the inside phone.

'*Si*,' he said, and she took it from him, realising that Felicita had probably left the building by now anyway.

'Hello?' she said into the mouthpiece—and was shocked and furious at one and the same time. For her caller was none other than Max!

'Hello, Elyn,' he said evenly, nothing in his tone to denote that the last time she had seen him she'd done her best to physically flatten him. 'I should very much like to see you,' he, to her absolute astonishment, went on quietly. The nerve of him! 'If you could come to my home...' That was as far as she allowed him to get.

What the hell did he think she was? No doubt, given the chance, the next thing would be that he'd be suggesting she ask Felicita to give her a lift! But he wasn't going to get that chance, because suddenly an explosion of emotions imploded in Elyn. 'No doubt you can't get here to see me because of your sprained ankle!' she erupted, and, not waiting to hear what he made of that, she slammed the phone down hard. She was still anywhere but in the computer-room when she came to to realise she had her bag in her hand. Belatedly, she remembered her manners. 'Thank you,' she murmured to the person whose phone she had used, and to Tino, 'I'll see you,' she said vaguely, collected her jacket, and got out of there.

The first thing she did on reaching the apartment was to phone about a flight home. The next thing she did was to pack and to ensure that she left the apartment as spick and span as she had found it. She debated long and hard about whether or not to leave a note at Zappelli Internazionale on her way to the airport—but who would she address it to? Certainly not Max, and though she honestly owned that she still liked Felicita, for the moment her wounds were too raw for her to feel like writing to her. Who, then? Tino? She decided against it. It just wasn't on for Tino to be the one to pass on the message that she had left.

It was just after five when Paolo, the hall porter on duty, phoned up to say that the taxi she had ordered was there. Elyn carried her luggage from the apartment, turned round to lock up—then realised that she couldn't very well take the key back to England with her.

That matter was solved when she handed Paolo a tip for carrying her luggage out to the taxi; she also handed him the key to the apartment. She smiled in answer to his query in Italian about the key, and, having understood barely a word other than that he seemed to be asking what he should do with it, she got into the taxi and was on her way.

Given the one-hour time difference, she was back in England only half an hour after her flight had taken off. And she felt no better to be home. She reached Bovington, and as her taxi from the station wound its way round its streets she observed that, while there had been an enormous change in her in the small time she had been away, Bovington had changed not at all.

She let herself into the house, knowing it was pointless to wish things back the way they had been before she had so crassly fallen in love with Max. She *had* fallen in love with him, and no amount of wishing was going to alter that.

Her mother and stepfather were out, so too was Loraine, Elyn discovered when she hefted her large suitcase into the hall, and her stepbrother came out to see who had arrived.

'Hello!' he exclaimed warmly, coming over to give her a brotherly kiss and a hug, showing not a sign of the angry person he'd been when she had told him she was going to Italy—right into the 'enemy camp' he had called it then, she remembered. 'Why didn't you let us know you were coming?' he questioned as they strolled into the drawing-room. 'I'd have met you at the airport.'

'That's sweet of you, Guy,' she smiled, 'I—er—wasn't sure myself until this morning that I'd be coming home today.' Quickly she changed the subject. 'I'm going to make a cup of coffee; would you like one?'

'Mmm, please,' he accepted, and Elyn left him and made for the kitchen, relieved to note from its homely but immaculate condition that they still had dear Madge with them.

The housekeeper was off duty, though, and was off on her own pursuits, and Elyn had the kitchen to herself, with Max in her thoughts and tears in her heart as she busied herself with the coffee.

How long did this heartache go on for? she wondered as she carried a tray from the kitchen to the drawing-room. Her love was so new, and so bruised—how long did it take for those wounds to heal and for one's private thoughts to centre on something else?

'Coffee!' she announced brightly as she returned to the drawing-room and set the tray down. 'Where is everybody, by the way?'

'The parents are at the theatre in Bovington, and Loraine's out with this new chap of hers—heaven help us!'

From that Elyn guessed that Guy endorsed her
mother's opinion of Loraine's latest. 'So how about
you?' she asked him, and, recalling her last telephone
conversation with her mother when she'd said that
Loraine had brought home another unsuitable type, Elyn
also recalled how her mother had said that Guy was
looking around for a job. 'Mother mentioned that you
were considering offering the workforce your services,'
she teased.

'I—er—had an interview only on Friday, as a matter
of fact,' he told her, but he seemed so sheepish suddenly
that Elyn just knew, since he was such an 'out in the
open' kind of person, that there was more to it than
that.

'Sounds interesting,' she remarked. 'What sort of a
job?'

Again she was struck by his slightly shamefaced
manner—but only began to suspect the reason for it
when, he answered, 'My—own line.'

'Designing? For ceramics?' she questioned.

'Got it in one.'

'Where?' she fired at him, but unless he was leaving
home to work away, then since there was only one 'fine
china' manufacturer in the area, she knew just where he
had applied.

'Zappelli Fine China,' Guy said swiftly, as though
needing to get it said and done quickly. 'I know, I know,'
he hurried on when, even though she was prepared for
it, Elyn couldn't help a start of surprise, 'I know I've
got a nerve after the hard time I gave you when you went
to work there, but although it's taken me longer to see
sense, I've discovered I'm at my happiest when I'm
working. Anyway, Zappelli's were advertising, and I went
on Friday and Brian Cole in the design section—do you
know him?' he broke off to ask.

'Yes, I know him,' said Elyn, and the rest of the design
team—and they knew her!

'Well, anyway, he's a sound sort of chap, and I thought we got on well. He certainly seemed to like the couple of examples of my work that I took along. Anyhow, he showed me round—they've got some fantastic equipment there,' he broke off to enthuse, 'so...'

'You—er—sound a bit keen,' Elyn commented. She hadn't seen Guy so alive and eager for ages.

'You could say that,' he grinned.

'And what did your father say when you told him?' she asked.

'Ah, well,' Guy said with another grin. 'You rather broke the ice there—thanks very much——' he inserted '—by going to work at Zappelli's first. I suppose I can say that you absorbed most of the flak, and that by the time my turn came Dad had mellowed somewhat. Did you know that he's thinking, seriously thinking, of selling Pillingers—the buildings, the land, the lot?'

'No!' she gasped.

'Straight up,' Guy assured her. 'Though I think I see your mother's hand in it somewhere—brochures for world cruises having been arriving daily.'

'Grief!' Elyn exclaimed, and after some moments of taking that in, 'So Sam's accepted the way things are,' she commented softly.

'And the way things have to be,' agreed her step-brother, going on, 'Anyway, he took my news about trying for Zappelli's far better than I'd expected. Though he did try to look stern as he told me that if it weren't for the fact that he's got nothing to leave me, he'd dis-inherit me.' Elyn smiled; she could see Sam saying it.

'So you think your interview went well?' she asked. She hadn't known that there was a vacancy in the design department, or she'd maybe have found a way of tact-fully suggesting he apply for it.

'I think so. He introduced me to the rest of the team, anyhow, and I don't think he'd have done that had there been no chance.'

'You already knew Hugh Burrell, though,' Elyn commented.

'Does he work there?' Guy seemed surprised, then shrugged. 'He must have been out somewhere,' he commented, and went on, 'Brian Cole had one or two others to interview, so he said, but he's going to let me know as soon as he can.' And, with another huge grin, 'I say, if I do get the job, we can go into work together. I can drive you in and...' Something in her expression caused him to break off. 'What's...?' he began, and Elyn knew this was something she could not keep to herself.

'I—er—don't work for Max Zappelli any more,' she said flatly, just Max's name on her lips making her feel wobbly inside.

'You don't! How come?'

Grief! Families! she sighed. Nothing was sacred. She didn't want to answer. But Guy was waiting, and he'd had a rotten time of it, and she loved him too. How come? There was no way to dress it up. 'I—er—walked out,' she said flatly.

'You walked out!' Guy exclaimed, appalled. 'For heaven's sake, when—why?'

When, was easier to answer. 'This morning,' she told him.

'Without giving notice?'

'I—was—er—cross about something,' she excused herself.

'*Cross*! Oh, Elyn! How *could* you?'

'How could I?' she blinked. Was this the same young man who'd joined in the general harangue when she told them she'd applied for a job at Zappelli's?

Guy did not answer her bounced-back question, but his expression suddenly went from grinning to defeated. 'Well, that's it! I might just as well forget that I ever had that interview last Friday!'

'How do you make that out?' she asked.

'Simple! My interview with Brian Cole was taken up solely with the job. But I was interviewed first by some bod named Nickson from Personnel. When I mentioned that I'd got a stepsister who was employed by them and gave your name, Nickson straight away remembered you. I thought he'd warmed to me from that point on, but I wish now that I'd kept quiet about you—at least that would have left me in there with a chance. Once word gets in from Italy—and it'll only take a minute to send a fax from Personnel to Personnel—that you...'

'You think my walking out has ruined your chances?'

'Don't you?' Guy tossed back gloomily. 'A fine impression for reliability our family will have made, with you walking out like that!'

'You're exaggerating,' Elyn argued faintly, though, as she thought about it, there was already suspicion hanging over her head about that missing design without having another black mark against her for leaving the firm's employ without giving proper notice. Oh, Lord, perhaps Guy was right, and it would have been far better for his prospect of employment with the firm had he not owned to having her for a stepsister. Add to that the fact that she had taken a swipe at the owner of the whole shoot— not that she could regret that—but, even given Guy's tremendous ability, it did not augur at all well for him.

She looked over at his despondent expression, and felt pulled in two about the normally good and gentle person he was. No way did she want to go anywhere near any firm that Max owned ever again. Against that, though, it was a certainty that Max would be spending most of this week—when, she winced, he wasn't holed up with Felicita—in Rome. Elyn had no idea if he had any plans to visit England after that, but, for Guy's sake, would it matter? Couldn't she, for her stepbrother's sake, go into the office tomorrow and, while at the same time keeping her ear to the ground for news of Max visiting the place, work out her resignation? Certainly he wouldn't come seeking her out; certainly, if she knew he was there, she'd make darned certain that she kept out of his way.

'Smile, sunshine,' she told her stepbrother quickly before she could change her mind. 'So I'll report at Zappelli, Pinwich, tomorrow, and do the decent thing.'

'Decent thing?' questioned Guy, starting to look hopeful.

'I'll formally resign—and work my notice out. Will that help, do you think?'

'Would you?' he asked eagerly.

'I haven't anything else to do,' she smiled.

'Oh, thanks, you're a pal, Elyn,' he declared, and she knew why she loved him like a brother when he added, 'You don't have to, you know.' And, 'What was it that made you so cross you felt you had to walk out?' he asked.

'Nothing that you need trouble your pretty little head about,' she teased, and he had just whacked a cushion at her, when their parents came home.

Elyn went to bed that night having been greeted by her mother and stepfather in astonishment at seeing her home, but having been able to conceal from them the inner torment she was enduring. In her room, though, with no need to pretend any more, she collapsed on to her bed and felt exhausted. She tried to put Max completely out of her thoughts—oh, that it was so easy! Though, with the anguish of love tearing her to shreds, it gave her little chance to fret too deeply about putting in an appearance, an unexpected appearance, at Zappelli Fine China tomorrow.

'Why, hello, Elyn!' her two assistants chorused in surprise when they arrived at the office they all shared the next morning.

'Good morning, Diana, Neil,' Elyn smiled.

'We weren't expecting you back yet!' Neil exclaimed, adding to warm her heart, 'But I'm glad you are. I need your instruction on several points.'

'Me too!' added Diana.

'If you can get them ready, I'll be back in ten minutes,' Elyn told them, but refrained from telling them that she was on her way to the Personnel department.

'Elyn!' Chris Nickson exclaimed, the moment he saw her. 'What are you doing here?' His greeting was so delighted that by then she was beginning to have real regrets that she had to leave. But, for her own peace of mind, she had to go through with it. In giving four weeks' notice there lay a risk, slight though she would make it, of seeing Max if he happened to come over. But she had to leave—if indeed, after yesterday's walk-out, she wasn't pushed.

'Hello, Chris,' she smiled, and, wanting this interview over, 'I know I wasn't expected today, but I've decided to leave, and I felt I'd rather work out my notice in England.'

For a few surprised seconds he stared at her, then, 'Take a seat,' he invited, 'and tell me what brought this on.' And five minutes later Elyn had finally convinced him that her 'personal reasons' for leaving were so strong that there was nothing he could do or say that could persuade her to change her mind. 'We'll be sorry to see you go, Elyn,' he accepted at last. 'None more so than me,' he added sincerely.

'Thank you, Chris,' she said, and stood up.

He walked to the door with her. 'I hope those "personal reasons" don't mean you're going to go back on your word to have dinner with me?' he questioned.

'Of course not,' she said at once, but found she wasn't feeling ready to date anyone just yet, so she hastily tacked on, 'But I'm a bit—er—preoccupied this week.'

'Then I shall be in touch with you first thing next Monday,' he grinned.

Elyn returned to her office, but could not settle. There was a restlessness in her, a yearning to be, not there, but back in Italy. Even as she repeated over and over again that she had done the only thing possible, and that it was ridiculous to want to be back in Italy, she could not help but want to be back.

She tried to throw herself into some work, but again and again she would find she had drifted off and had her head filled with thoughts of Max again. He would be in Rome for sure by now.

On Wednesday not only was he constantly in her head, but she began to feel jumpy each time the internal phone rang in case it might be Chris Nickson to say he'd had orders from Italy to dismiss her.

When on Thursday Chris Nickson did ring through, at first she nearly died from the embarrassment of it. Consequently her thoughts were in turmoil when it turned out that his reason for contacting her was not to ask her to go and see him, but to tell her, 'I know you said you were a bit preoccupied this week, but I've just been given a couple of theatre tickets for tonight, and I wondered if...'

Elyn replaced her phone a minute later, and a minute after that realised she had just accepted an invitation to the theatre that evening! Well, it was too late now to do anything about it, she decided. And anyway, she lied to herself, perhaps an evening out might make her feel better.

The play might have been good; Elyn owned she was having difficulty in giving it her full concentration. Which was perhaps why she showed more enthusiasm than she felt to counteract that when Chris suggested that they go for a Chinese meal. 'Anywhere else will be closed by now,' he explained.

'I love Chinese,' she declared, and saw that Chris looked pleased that the evening was being extended.

He wasn't Max, but he was very pleasant, though, since what they had most in common was their place of work, a good deal of their conversation revolved around Zappelli Fine China.

But while Elyn desperately wanted to ask Chris if he knew how her stepbrother's job application was progressing, she was torn between the ethics of asking, and the certainty that Guy would be put out if she let this opportunity go by.

Families! she thought again, but she loved hers. She felt warmer towards Chris too when, having discussed a few aspects of his work, just as if he had read her thoughts, he commented, 'You knew your stepbrother had applied for a job in the design section?'

'I've been afraid to ask about it,' she smiled, 'but I'm bursting to know if I can pass on some good news,' she added openly.

Hopefully she waited, but as Chris stared at her and she realised that perhaps she had just overstepped the bounds of friendship, to her great surprise he didn't follow up what she had said, but, his eyes still on her, he exclaimed, 'You really are quite astonishingly beautiful!' Oh, heavens, Elyn thought, flattered, but not sure how she felt if his compliment was a prelude to him wanting to become more friendly. But she didn't have to employ any backing-away tactics, she found, for a second later his intent gaze altered, and he was teasing, 'You didn't come out with me just to find out how your stepbrother's interview with Brian Cole went, did you?'

'Good heavens, no!' she exclaimed. But she relaxed and smiled when she could see he was teasing, and joked back, 'Not that I wouldn't have put in a good word for him with Brian had I known he had a vacancy in his section.'

'Didn't you know? Of course you didn't! It was a nine days' wonder at the time. But...' Chris thought for a moment, then ended '... it must have happened on the afternoon before you flew out to Italy the next morning. It was, I remember now, because you cancelled our date for that evening. I . . .'

'Chris,' Elyn stopped him before he should muddle her further, 'switch the light on.'

'Switch . . .' he broke off, and as it clicked that she was asking him to put some light on what he was saying, 'My apologies, Elyn. Shall I go back to the beginning?'

'It might help.'

'Hugh Burrell——' he began.

'He works in the design section,' she said, to let him know she was now on his wavelength.

'Not any more, he doesn't.'

'He doesn't?' she exclaimed. 'He's left?'

'Helped on his way,' Chris explained. 'Though to be more accurate, he was given instant dismissal.'

'Instant dismissal!' she gasped, and as what else he had said about it happening that afternoon—that never-to-be-forgotten afternoon—prior to her going to Italy the following day, started to sink in, she just *knew* it had to have something to do with that missing design. 'Did *he* steal that design?' she asked shakenly.

'You knew about it?' Chris asked, and when she nodded, to her gratitude he didn't question how she had known when, until it was all out in the open, no one else had, but answered, 'Yes, he took it. Though he hadn't managed to get it off the premises when it was found.'

'It's been found!' she echoed, and Chris nodded.

'It's my guess that he was waiting for things to cool—security was instantly if discreetly stepped up when that valuable design went missing,' he inserted.

'Where was it?' she asked.

'He'd hidden it at the back of a solid, very full and therefore immovable cabinet in Brian's office—the last place anyone would think to look.'

'Only somebody did?'

'Security,' he explained. 'It seems the design was a rather large piece of work, so that, in the time allowed, it seemed unlikely it could have been got out of the building. While Security kept discreet surveillance for the rest of that day, a thorough search was instigated that night.' Chris broke off. 'Honestly, it's so like something out of a spy film that I'm still blinking myself! Since they still didn't know who took it, though, hidden cameras were placed in Brian's office.'

'Good heavens!' Elyn gasped. 'They caught Hugh Burrell when he went to get it?'

'They caught him on film going straight to the immovable cabinet and checking the back to see if it was still there.'

'And was it?'

'It had been substituted, but he didn't know that when he half pulled it out, smiled, and pushed it back again,' he replied, but already a sick feeling inside Elyn was making her feel quite ill, and other questions were queueing up to be asked.

'Did—er—Mr Zappelli know all this was going on?' she asked, every scrap of brain power telling her that he must have known—only she didn't want to believe it.

'Oh yes,' Chris smiled. 'You might say he directed operations.'

Elyn drew a steadying breath. 'So he knew that afternoon, that Tuesday before I went to Italy on the Wednesday, that Hugh Burrell was the guilty party?'

'I'll say he did! He flew in specially from Italy that day, especially for the purpose of interviewing him. It was Mr Zappelli who dismissed him from the company, Mr Zappelli who, that Tuesday afternoon, personally sacked him.'

Elyn lay sleepless in her bed that night, too furious for sleep. That Max could do that to her! Could, all this time, when he knew that she was innocent of any crime, string her along and let her believe her honesty was still in doubt. He had kissed her—and she—she had *let* him! My stars, garrotting was too good for him!

By morning her fury had simmered down to ice-cold anger—and hurt. Damn him, it was plain that she still loved the treacherous swine, or she wouldn't feel that pain, she acknowledged as she went down to a breakfast she didn't want, but which would be preferable to her family asking where she was and what was the matter.

'Maybe I'll hear today!' Guy said hopefully as he joined her in the breakfast-room.

'Er—yes,' she said vaguely, then realised that he must be talking about his job application. Then she began to feel guilty that, in the first instance, what Chris had revealed last night had taken completely out of her head all idea of sounding him out about Guy's chances, and in the second instance, that she might yet snooker any chance Guy had.

She had not had any intention of going anywhere near Zappelli Fine China that day. But suddenly she was thrown into a dilemma. Max had once said to her, 'I hope I'm fairer than that.' But, given that she had hit him, given that she had walked out of Zappelli Internazionale and had flown home, did the fact that he had continued to allow her to think there was some doubt about her honesty, or the fact that she had turned up at Zappelli Fine China to resign and work out her notice go for nothing? The way she equated it, she was more owed than owing, but would she end her stepbrother's hopes if she didn't honour her four weeks' notice?

'I'm doing nothing special this morning,' Guy suddenly broke into her thoughts. 'I'll drive you into Pinwich, if you like.'

She looked at him and, feeling never more dejected, knew she just wasn't up to the hassle should she tell Guy she wasn't going to work at Zappelli's again. Damn Max Zappelli. Damn him. Damn him to hell!

She was still damning the man she loved. Still trying to get him and his treachery out of her head. Still trying to get some troublesome figures to behave when at three thirty-five that afternoon, for the moment the sole occupant of the office, she had to break off in mid-calculation to answer the incessant clamouring of the internal phone.

'Yes!' she said, her tone coming out more sharply than she had meant it to—and nearly fell off her chair in astonishment.

'My office, Miss Talbot, *now*!' rapped a voice she would know anywhere, and bang, the phone went dead.

Stunned, disbelieving, Elyn stared at the phone in her hand. Had she imagined it? Did she have Max so much on her mind that she had imagined that call? But she couldn't have—she still held the phone in her hand. And suddenly everything went wild inside her.

Max was here! He was here, in Pinwich! In this very building! He should, by rights, be in Rome. But he wasn't in Rome—he was here!

CHAPTER NINE

MAX was here—here in Pinwich! Not only that, but
wanting to see her. Was actually waiting to see her!
Waiting for her to go along and present herself at his
office!

Elyn was in a flat spin for several minutes, and those
minutes seemed like an age as she struggled to pull herself
together. I'm not going! she decided, and as she looked
round for her bag, which was precisely where she always
kept it, going home seemed to her to be a much better
idea.

She grabbed up her bag, ready to flee, when two things
stopped her. Oh, grief, Guy! Belatedly she thought of
Guy and how he would react if she went home early and
told him that she had, after all, walked out. Though she
felt more like running out than walking. But—she
wavered—hadn't she run enough?

Elyn sat down, unaware that she had sprung to her
feet. Why run just because Max wanted to see her? And
for that matter, what did he want to see her about? For
that matter too, what did he think he could say that could
possibly interest her?

Suddenly, though, at the thought that maybe he intended to sack her personally, the way he had personally
dismissed Hugh Burrell, Elyn found the stiffening she
needed. Let him try, she fumed, starting to get angry,
and Guy or no Guy, she would tell him exactly what he
could do with his job!

Her stiffening, her anger, stayed with her right up until
she reached his office door. 'Come in!' she heard his

voice respond to her tap at his door—and her legs went weak.

She squared her shoulders, took a steadying breath and reached for the door-handle. She might be shaking like a leaf inside, but only she was going to know it.

An unexpected wave of tender emotion rushed over her as she opened the door and stepped into Max's office. Tall, straight and unsmiling, he was standing to one side of the settee in the room, his eyes watching the door. And oh, how dear he was to her!

Elyn closed the door and strove hard to hold down the emotion that was trying to trip her up. 'You wished to see me, Mr Zappelli?' she queried. Mr Zappelli? To this man who had so tenderly held her in his arms last Saturday? To this man who so tenderly, and in turns so passionately, kissed her? *And*, prodded that part of her that she sorely needed, who had secretly acted so treacherously to her.

She caught his sharp look on her and knew that he wasn't too much taken with her tone. But she was fighting for survival, and she didn't care what he was or was not taken with. She wanted this interview over— wanted to be gone.

'Take a seat!' he instructed shortly, his dark eyes taking in her smart emerald suit and crisp white shirt. 'Not there!' he rapped, when she would have gone over to the high-backed chair by his desk and pointed to one of the easy-chairs in the room.

Elyn shrugged. He was the boss—for the moment. She looked away from him and went to take the seat he had indicated, and when she raised her head, she saw that he had taken the pace necessary round the settee, and was now seated too.

Neatly, decorously, she crossed her ankles and sat with her long legs to one side, trying to appear casual. But it was unnerving to have Max say nothing, just giving her that hard, steady scrutiny—almost, she thought ridiculously, as if he was unnerved too, and hardly knew where to begin.

But, to show just exactly how ridiculous that thought was, only a moment later Max touched a hand to his chin and coolly, levelly, questioned, 'Why did you leave Italy in such a rush, Elyn?'

She could have done without the 'Elyn'. To have him 'Miss Talbot' her through the whole of this interview would have suited her far better. Just to be called 'Elyn' in that naturally seductive voice of his was making a nonsense of her trying to pull herself together.

Had she foreseen this interview she would have had something rehearsed. But she hadn't for a second thought that should Max come to England—especially today, when he should still be in Rome—he would invite this interview.

'I'd decided to leave!' she stated off the top of her head. 'It seemed to me to be a waste of company money for Tino to continue to use his valuable time in giving me any further training when I would be leaving.'

'Mmm,' Max commented, stroking a reflective hand over his strong and manly chin. 'That was very fair of you.' She relaxed a fraction. Good, he had swallowed it! 'If,' he went on, fixing her with a dark assessing gaze, 'not exactly truthful.'

'What do you mean?' she fired, striving not to panic, agitation filling her as she realised she shouldn't have relaxed a fraction, not one iota, where this man was concerned.

He moved one shoulder expressively, but his gaze was as intent as ever. 'What I mean,' he replied, 'is that either you lied to Felicita Rocca when you said you merely wanted a transfer to England, or you are lying to me now.' Oh, lord, he was much too smart for her! 'Why, Elyn, I wonder,' he went on relentlessly, 'do you find it necessary to lie to me?'

With her feelings of agitation peaking, hot words rushed to her lips to deny that she was lying. Suddenly, though, she came to a full stop. Dammit! Who the hell did he think he was, to push her into a corner after the way *he* had *lied* to *her*!

'I might ask you the same question?' she tilted her stubborn chin to bounce back at him. She was leaving anyway; let him sack her for impudence, see if she cared!

She thought, momentarily, that he looked a shade put off of his stride, but he nodded, and responded coolly, 'I can explain, in due time, why I had to pretend I had injured myself on that mountain.'

The nerve of him, that he could so blatantly bring that up! But Elyn didn't want him referring to anything to do with those twenty-four hours they had shared in the Dolomites, and determinedly, if with her insides turning, she stayed steadfastly on the tack she wanted to be on.

'I wasn't meaning *that*!' she retorted snappily. 'I was meaning that out-and-out lie you told me when I asked if the person who stole Brian Cole's precious design had been found.'

'Ah!' he murmured, paused, and, as if it was dragged from him, 'I was hoping you might still be in ignorance of it.'

'I'll bet you were!' she flew, it was all too much that he could say what he had, could openly, unblushingly own that he still hoped she was in ignorance of all suspicion being removed from her! 'Thanks for nothing!' she seethed, and was on her feet, storming to the door.

She had her hand on the door-handle ready to wrench it open when, 'Elyn! Don't leave!' rent the air.

Her hand froze; she froze. But then she remembered that she'd heard him say something similar before. At Cavalese, last Sunday! 'You can't leave,' he had said, and, when there had been nothing in the world the matter with his foot, he had pretended he needed her help.

My stars! What an idiot she'd been then! But never again. Oh, no, never again! Swiftly she spun round, hot words already pouring from her. 'Your foot, is it?' she stormed with furious sarcasm. 'Your poor injured...' She broke off. Max, some of his colour gone, was holding on to—the settee! 'What's the matter—what's wrong?' she demanded urgently, shocked and shaken, for, as she had sprung to her feet, so too, as if he would charge after her, had Max—and it seemed as though that action had hurt. Somehow, he appeared to be actually rocking, unbalanced, where he stood!

He was putting it on! She refused to believe that he was injured in some way. But even so, when he said not a word, when she knew what a lying rat he was, she just had to go back further into the room. Warily, she walked slowly round him to the other side of the settee. She stared at him, at the way he was proudly trying to appear as if there was nothing wrong with him—but there was! Her eyes travelled over him, down to his feet—and then she saw it. Protruding from beneath the settee, as if he had been trying to hide it, she saw a rubber ferrule.

She went over to it, took hold of it and pulled—it was attached to a walking stick. 'What's this?' she demanded, and wasn't sure she would not have brained him with it had he answered, 'A walking stick'.

Solemnly his dark eyes stayed steady on her mistrusting green ones. 'Some woman, in a magnificent fury, hurled a ski-boot at me,' he quietly let fall.

Startled, shocked again, she stared at him. 'It hit you!' she exclaimed.

'It did,' he agreed in the same quiet tone. 'It hit me, bounced off and, while I was coming after you at a run, I tripped over it—and twisted my ankle.' Elyn's breath caught. 'If you'd like proof, and I'd hardly blame you,' he conceded, 'I'll willingly take off the strapping to show you the swelling and the bruising. Though I wouldn't

mind at all if we could finish saying all we've got to say
to each other sitting down.'

Her heart somersaulted. His tone was milder, kinder
and, she had to own, his pain was her pain, for to know
she had incapacitated him made her feel dreadful. His
words 'all we've got to say to each other', though, were
making her wary again. There was nothing more she had
to say to him... But suddenly the look of strain on his
face touched her, and involuntarily she pleaded, 'Oh,
do sit down, Max.'

A trace of a smile appeared on his up to now unsmiling mouth, and Elyn was a mass of agitation inside
again. 'After you,' he suggested, and while praying that
she had not given away the extent of her caring, Elyn
was able to hide her expression from him by going back
to take the chair she had so hurriedly vacated.

He was sitting on the settee again too by the time she
looked up, his colour returning. But by then she had got
herself a little more under control. 'You must have fallen
very heavily,' she looked across at him to comment
coolly.

'It seemed so at the time,' he replied, his eyes on her,
not seeming to miss a thing.

'What did you do?' she questioned, and as she imagined the whole ghastly scene of Max fallen in a heap
and maybe unable to get up, 'You should have telephoned me at my hotel, I'd have...' She broke off,
damning her impetuous tongue.

'You'd have what?' he took up, another endearing hint
of a smile coming to his mouth. 'From the whirlwind
way you left, I rather thought "Go to hell" might be
the best reception any phone call about my hurt foot
might receive.'

'You—er—could be right there,' she allowed, and
didn't want him kind or smiling; it made a nonsense of
all her attempts to be anti for more than two minutes
together. 'So presumably, since you couldn't drive...'

'Couldn't drive, couldn't walk, and, not to overstress the situation, I just could not believe that, so instantly, I was totally incapacitated!'

Oh, Max! she could have cried for him. But she mustn't be soft—that way led to disaster, to letting this perceptive man see that when he bled, she bled; when he hurt, so too did she hurt. 'So you rang elsewhere for help?' she suggested.

'I contacted a doctor.'

'And?' she questioned. It was like pulling teeth to get all the details out of him!

'From there hospital, X-rays, and my home by ambulance.'

Oh, Max, my poor dear love! her heart cried in horror. 'But you haven't broken anything?'

'To my surprise, no,' he replied, that hint of a smile coming out again, while from that 'To my surprise' Elyn guessed that it hurt enough for him to have broken every bone in his foot.

'That's good,' she murmured—a polite enough thing to say, she thought, and a comment that gave away nothing of how she felt inside.

'And that,' Max took up, his eyes gentle on her face, 'considering my lies to you, my deception, is more than generous of you, Elyn.'

Don't—oh, please don't, she wanted to cry, her spine already starting to melt at his gentle look. 'So an ambulance took you home,' she managed to find a degree of stiffening from somewhere.

'From where I telephoned you on Monday and said that I wanted to see you—and, for my pains, received another helping of your most ferocious temper.'

'What did you expect?' she asked, remembering Monday all too clearly. But she remembered too her jealousy over Felicita—entirely unwarranted, she could see that now—but by no chance did she want this clever man to know of the uproar her emotions had been in at that time. The time now seemed right to change the subject. 'I'm not certain why you asked me to come to see you—er—today, now, I mean, not then.' Oh, grief, she was making a real hash of it! 'But,' she forged gamely on, and even found a spark of spirit, 'if you've now changed your mind about being happy to leave me in ignorance about that missing design, and have now decided to condescend——' she found some sarcasm for good measure ' —to let me breathe a sigh of relief that there's no longer a shadow hanging over my good name, then I hope you're not expecting me to thank you for it!'

'No, I'm not expecting that,' he agreed, his eyes on the sparking anger that suddenly flashed in her green eyes.

'Good!' she snapped, and since that must be it, she started to get up from her chair.

'*No!*' Max stopped her, and as she stared at him, she realised that he must have more to say, but that, her language not being his language, he must be sorting through for the best way to say what he had to say.

And, as Elyn faced the fact that she didn't want to go, not yet, that she loved him and wanted to hear what he had to say, be it only that he wanted her to work out her notice in Italy, she subsided back into her chair.

She had just decided though that, love him with all her heart as she might, she could just not see the point of working out her notice in Italy, when, to confound her utterly, Max began, 'To confess to you my lie with regard to that missing design is part of why I've asked you to come and see me, but only a small part.' And, as she stared at him, 'There is more to it than that.' He seemed to hesitate, but that gentle note was back in his voice again when, he added softly, 'More Elyn, between us, than that.'

Oh, heavens, she needed help from somewhere. But she was being seduced by his tone, and couldn't think clearly. 'Oh, yes?' she murmured enquiringly, and hoped she was the only one who would notice that her voice had gone husky. She coughed to clear a small constriction, and found a bit more backbone. 'How—er— do you make that out?' she queried. 'I mean, if you're referring to work, then . . .'

'I'm not referring to work, *cara*,' he butted in quietly, and Elyn's backbone was on the melt again.

'Well—er—there c-can't be anything of any significance, any importance, any. . .' Her voice dried, and she had to give another nervous little cough before she could go on again. 'If you're talking about friendship——' Oh lord, was she making a complete fool of herself? Was he not meaning that at all? She swallowed hard. 'Well then, in my book, friendship is based on trust. And you, Max Zappelli,' she snatched at another passing strand of backbone, 'I wouldn't trust an inch!'

There, if he'd any inkling that she cared for him, she reckoned she just sent such a notion flying. But strangely, when she had expected him to come over all proud Italian, to start Miss Talboting her for her nerve, and to deliver a one-line dismissal, to her amazement he did nothing of the kind. But, leaning back on the settee, one immaculately suited fine wool sleeve relaxed and easy on the settee arm, he looked at her expressive face for some long quiet moments, then stated quietly, 'You are beautiful, Elyn, quite stunning, and, I can see—a mass of nerves.'

'I'm not!' she denied before he'd barely got the words out of his mouth.

'You are, and I've wronged you, and I want to put it right—and,' he added, with a smile that nearly sank her, 'I confess that I am nervous too.'

'You? What have you got to be nervous about?' she questioned, and could have bitten out her tongue, because implicit in her question somewhere was confirmation that she was indeed nervous herself!

If Max had noticed it, though, he gave no sign but, leaning forward, his seemingly relaxed manner gone, 'There is so much I want from you, for you, for us,' he told her, and while Elyn stared at him, hardly crediting what she was hearing, 'so much I want—but first and most important of all, I want that trust you spoke of just now.'

I'll bet you do, Elyn thought, staring at him, barely able to believe, if her brain hadn't totally deserted her, that Max had just propositioned her! She had been his for the taking up at that chalet! He had rejected her then, but now, it seemed, had changed his mind and decided he would quite like an affair after all!

'You've some plan already worked out on how to go about gaining that trust, of course?' she questioned sarcastically, while part of her warned that she should get out now. She was vulnerable where he was concerned, for heaven's sake. Get up, Elyn. Get up, and walk away before it's too late! Before he mesmerises you into doing all that he asks.

'I've no plan.' Max ignored her sarcasm—indeed, she realised, he appeared to know so much about her, he seemed to expect it. More, he had decided to bury his pride and take it—take whatever she threw at him. Heaven help her, did he want her in his bed so badly? She couldn't work it out. She had been his for the taking once, but... 'I've no plan,' he repeated firmly, 'other than to tell you the whole truth.'

'That will make a refreshing change!' she erupted briefly to toss in sarcastically.

But again he weathered her sarcasm, and even smiled a gentle smile as he assured her, 'Believe me, my dear, I'm not usually a liar.' Elyn was drowning from that 'my dear' and was instructing her legs to move and get going while she still could, but then Max added, 'So you see what, almost from my first sight of you, you have done to me.'

She had done to *him*? It was too late, she couldn't move. She shot a glance at him—his look was sincere— and she, even though her brain if not her heart shouted that she was being foolish, had to stay.

'Er—I'm afraid I—er—don't...' Her husky voice faded.

But Max seemed encouraged. 'If you do not understand me, *cara*, I am not surprised,' he murmured softly. 'For I confess to you that there have been many times since I have met you when I have not understood myself.'

'Oh?' she struggled, and felt not a scrap clearer.

'Perhaps if I explain how, from that first moment of meeting you in that doorway, in this building, you were in and out of my thoughts, you will begin to understand.'

Elyn remembered, oh, so clearly, her first meeting with him. Her insides had started to misbehave from that very moment, she recalled. From that moment she had felt vulnerable where he was concerned, even though she had denied it at the time. But that he too, so he said, had been affected by that unexpected meeting... She just *had* to hear more, question more.

'I was... You said I was in and out of your thoughts?' she queried.

He nodded. 'At first I told myself that it was purely because it is rare—that is to say, it has never been known for any woman of my acquaintance to give me the haughty treatment, and to walk by without a word.'

'I'll bet!' She couldn't help the words that dropped so acidly from her lips.

To her annoyance, though, Max looked more pleased than put out. There was certainly a smile hovering on his mouth as he enquired softly, 'You are jealous, Elyn?'

'Hardly!' she denied disdainfully. He didn't look totally convinced, and she felt like hitting him—though she was not sufficiently annoyed to want to leave before she heard more. 'Are you saying it was not that I'd

walked on without a word that caused me to be—er—
in and out of your thoughts?'

'That is what I am saying,' he agreed. 'Can you not
pity me, little one, that from merely being in and out of
my thoughts, in a very short while you were more in
than out, until one day I suddenly found you had taken
up permanent residence there.'

'Oh!' she exclaimed. That was exactly how it was for
her, over him! But he couldn't be meaning *that*, could
he? Don't be ridiculous, snorted her brain—and gave
her wilting backbone the stiffening kick it needed. 'That's
why you thought it would be such good fun to have me
think you believed me a design thief, was it?' she
challenged.

'It wasn't like that!' he denied instantly.

'No? It is from where I see it!' She was at once alarmed
for him as much as for herself, when he made a
movement as if to get up and come over to her. 'I can
hear you quite well from there,' she told him in an urgent
spurt.

He looked defeated for a moment, but then suggested, 'You wouldn't consider coming over here, I
suppose?'

'Not a chance!'

'You are making matters very difficult for me, Elyn,
do you know that?'

'At the risk of instant dismissal,' she retorted, 'good!'

For long level moments Max studied her mutinous expression, then all at once his strained manner eased, and
he commented a little ruefully, 'Perhaps I should have
recognised the spirit in you, the trouble you would be
to me, the very first time I looked into those defiant and
fantastic green eyes.' And while Elyn's backbone became
so much water again, he was going on, 'But even had I
the sense to realise the anguish the haughty, finely dressed
woman who was apparently on my payroll would cause
me, I doubt if I could have acted any differently.'

Anguish! He probably meant pain and anguish from his foot, said her head. But, butted in her heart, her foolish heart, what if he didn't? Perhaps he meant something entirely different, her thoughts darted. 'You mean anguish about that missing design?' she made a choky stab.

Max gazed steadily at her for a moment, then murmured, 'Ah, that design. It was the start of my deception.' He followed on, 'Though at first, you, along with anyone else with access to Brian Cole's office, *were* a suspect.'

Elyn accepted that. 'Until the culprit was found—I'll go along with that,' she agreed.

'Thank you,' Max smiled, and went on to tell her how it had been from his side of it. 'Brian was in raptures about his design. With him in such high euphoria when he came to report, I told him not to bring it to me, but went with him to take a look at it.'

'But it wasn't there.'

'Not a sign of it!' Max smiled. 'Brian was in shock. It was his baby, his brain-child. He just couldn't believe it. He had left it on his desk—but it had gone.'

'Poor Brian!' Elyn sympathised.

'Naturally I had to start asking who, in the time he had come looking for me, and waited while I finished a phone call, had been to his office.'

'Hugh Burrell told you I'd been there, alone,' Elyn supplied.

Max nodded. 'I asked for your extension number and rang you—and just knew, when I heard your lovely voice, that it must belong to the arrogant woman I had met early that morning.'

'Did you?' she gasped, but pulled herself together to ask, 'So you weren't surprised when I walked in—even though you asked me if I was Elyn Talbot?'

'I could have been wrong.' Just his look said that he'd known he wasn't, and Elyn strove hard to get her mind back to what they had been talking about.

'You then proceeded to ask me about the missing design.'

'And was very soon discounting, from your open manner, that you could have anything to do with it.'

'Really?' she asked, astounded.

'Oh yes, *cara*,' he replied softly. 'I had to continue, of course. But the more and more everything seemed to point to you—there being no need for you to be there because you already had the figures you'd come for, the fact that you knew that a couple of members of the design staff wouldn't be there because you'd seen them at the tea dispenser; and above all, because of your connections with and for Pillingers, your knowledge of who would be likely to be in the market for such an item— the more convinced I became that it couldn't be you.'

Looking across at him, Elyn felt certain that he was telling the truth. But he had lied to her before, on this very same subject. 'Did you still feel that when at the end of that same working day you asked me to come and see you?' she questioned warily.

'I should continue to question you in the design section when Burrell was already rubbing his hands with glee at your discomfiture?'

'Oh, Max, you are kind!' she exclaimed in a moment of weakness. Hurriedly she pulled herself together again. 'Not that you were so kind when, a week later, you sent for me again! You knew *then*, for absolute positive certain, that I hadn't touched that design, that Hugh Burrell had, because you had personally dismissed him for that very reason, and——'

'Please try to understand, dear Elyn,' Max broke into what was becoming an angry tirade. 'I had been in Italy for a whole week with your face haunting me.' That stopped her in her tracks. 'When I had a call to say that

Burrell had been caught incriminatingly on film, I decided, when Brian Cole could have interrogated him and dismissed him as easily as I, that I must come to England and do the job myself.'

'Because—you f-felt it was your job to do it?' Elyn asked slowly.

'That, of course, is what I told myself,' Max agreed. 'But I later realised that to personally dismiss that apology for a man was just an excuse. In reality, I wanted to see you again.'

'Good heavens!' she whispered faintly.

'Which is why, once I had dealt with him, I asked you to come and see me. And when—please believe me, I'd fully intended to tell you how Burrell had removed that design more, I'm sorry to say, to make life difficult for you than to steal it, when you asked if I'd discovered who'd stolen it, to my amazement I heard myself answer, "Unfortunately not".'

Elyn was shaken that the grudge Hugh Burrell held against her extended that far, but that was not the issue. 'You had, until then, fully intended to tell me?' she pressed, somehow needing clarification.

'But yes, please believe me,' he confirmed.

'Then why...?' she began to question, feeling totally at a loss.

'A question I was to ask myself many times, but not find the answer to until much later. All I knew then was that I, who am not a liar, had lied. And that to cover that lie I was going to have to find a reason for calling you to my office.' He looked levelly at her for an unnerving second or two, then owned, 'I found that reason by looking at you and realising that with you there with me, so lovely, so honest, when I had to return to Italy to attend a function that evening, I wanted you to come with me.'

'You...I...' Elyn broke off as suddenly her brain began to work overtime. 'You demanded that I go to Italy for training,' she reminded him. 'You knew, because I'd slipped up and let you know how much I needed my salary, that there was no way I could refuse. But was it so absolutely essential that I fly out the next day—that night, if you'd had your way—for training?'

'What can I say?' Max gave a Latin shrug which she suddenly found most endearing. 'I wanted you where I could see you. My work is mainly in Verona, Italy, yours in Pinwich, England.' He grinned suddenly. 'It would not do, Elyn.'

She swallowed, and tried hard to keep what sense he had left her with. 'But...' Her voice failed, and she tried again. 'But all the while you let me believe you thought me a crook!' she protested.

'Oh, but no!' he denied. 'Maybe I never put it into words. But surely my actions...'

'Actions!' she cut in, and was glad to feel a spark of anger stirring. Grief, he'd be trampling all over her in a minute! 'Your actions spoke far louder than words!' she said hotly. 'Lying to me about Hugh Burrell not having been found out! G——'

'I've explained. I couldn't——'

'Getting me to fly out to Italy!' she refused to let him interrupt. But, as more of her brain power woke up, 'You had to fly me out, didn't you?' she snapped. 'Since the news that you'd kicked Hugh Burrell out on his ear was about to break at any moment, you knew that if you hadn't, if I'd stayed at my desk in England, there was no way I was not going to hear of it.'

'That is true,' he agreed at once. 'But I insist, although that of course did occur to me, that it was not my prime reason for my wanting you in Verona, where I could see you daily.'

Elyn stared at him belligerently. Though as she had for the moment run out of steam, the best she could come up with was a stubborn, 'But you didn't see me every day, did you?'

'Oh, Elyn, have you no idea what you have done to me?'

What Elyn did not need was that at his tone, his words, his look, her ridiculous heart should suddenly leap and that hope should enter the fray.

All anger suddenly departed, and she discovered that her voice was barely audible. 'No, I d-don't think I really do,' she told him.

'Oh, sweet Elyn!' he breathed, his look tender, his tone gentle. 'So clever with figures, yet you cannot, and have not yet, worked out—as I own I did not acknowledge myself until recently—why it is I wanted you with me. Why it is that I raced from the airport in Verona to the airport in Bergamo to meet your plane that early evening.'

Stunned for the moment, Elyn blinked. 'But you were on your way home when Felicita contacted you to say my flight had been diverted to...' she began.

'Because I shall never again lie to you,' Max interrupted warmly, 'I am admitting all lies now.'

'Oh,' she mumbled, not knowing where she was any more.

'I could not wait until the next day to see you,' he went on. 'Though I own I was not admitting that even to myself at that time when I decided I would be the one to meet your plane in Verona.' Elyn was still gulping at that as he continued, 'When my enquiries revealed that your plane was coming in at Bergamo, I raced from one airport to the other and, having not got my breath back from that, felt my heart ready to stop at the loveliness of you, and of your radiant smile, when you turned round and said, "Oh, hello".'

'Truly?' she gasped, her eyes saucer-wide.

'Truly,' he confirmed, and made her heart leap again when, after another gentle look at her, he added, 'Only much later was I able to realise that from that moment on all was lost for me.'

Hope, a gigantic hope, surged up in her, but she was feeling suddenly too tongue-tied to say anything more than a husky, 'You—er—drove me to the firm's apartment.'

'And had an evening appointment of long standing with some business people,' he revealed.

'You—er—didn't want—to leave?' she asked, having instant recall about everything to do with him, and remembering her feeling then that he had seemed reluctant to depart.

He nodded. 'And could not understand it,' he owned. 'Instincts of self-preservation, I believe, were responsible for my making sure our paths did not collide the following day. But,' he went on, his mouth picking up most devastatingly at the corners, 'that did not stop me from instructing Felicita—in the interests of your welfare, of course—to keep me informed about your activities, no matter how trivial she might assume those activities to be.'

'Good heavens!' Elyn gasped.

'As you say, *cara*, good heavens! I never thought, when she reported back to me that first Friday you were in Verona that you were planning to spend the weekend sightseeing, that you would be sightseeing anywhere but in Verona. Had I thought, had I known you were planning to go sightseeing in Bolzano, I'd have put a stop to that too!'

'Too? I don't——'

'Forgive me,' Max cut in, his dark eyes studying her face. 'Forgive the jealousy that raged in me when you told me you'd been to Bolzano.'

'You—were *jealous*?' Elyn asked incredulously.

'You had not been to Bolzano on your own, I knew,' he replied. 'I suspected you'd been with Tino Agosta. I had, I hoped, already put a stop to your dining with him that Friday night by inventing a bilingual secretary going home ill.'

'Inventing? But she did go home ill! I spent hour after hour typing out a report which you wanted urgently. A report which...'

'A report which Felicita had typed in Italian for me the day before, but which,' he confessed, 'I had no need to have typed in English at all.'

'But—but...' Elyn was reeling.

'But I was getting deeper and deeper into a mesh of lies,' Max took over. 'I enjoyed having you there in my office. Enjoyed watching how your sharp intelligence was taken with that report. I...' He broke off, then, looking directly into her eyes, 'Elyn—my dear, dear Elyn. You must by now, I think have used some of that sharp intelligence to have seen how it is with me.' She swallowed a lump in her throat, and he, intently watching her, smiled, then asked, 'Do you still insist, dear heart, on sitting over there?'

Oh, what was he saying? She knew what it sounded like he was saying, but it was all so unexpected, she couldn't be sure.

'Shall I come over to you?' he asked when she hadn't moved a muscle to come over to him. Indeed, she seemed welded to the spot.

He went to shift his position—but 'No, stay where you are!' she cried anxiously, fearful of the pressure he would place on his injured foot.

He sank back down again, but his eyes were fixed on her when quietly but firmly he asked, 'Are you going to come to me?'

'Wh-why should I?' she responded nervously—and clutched hard on to the arms of her chair at his reply.

'Because,' he said solemnly, sincerely, 'while I admit I have lied to you and have deceived you in the past, I am neither lying nor deceiving now when I tell you that I—love you very much, *amore mia*. That I love you with all my heart.'

'Oh, Max!' Elyn whispered, and at her tone, the emotion in her, he was no longer holding back, but was struggling to his feet as if to come to her. 'Oh, no, you'll hurt yourself!' she cried, and was out of her chair and going over to him.

She reached him just as he made it to his feet, and as his arms opened to her she went straight into them. She was aware of him crooning something in Italian in her ears. It sounded wonderful.

In his arms she wanted to be, and as her arms went around him that was how, locked together for an age, they stayed. Then, 'Let me look at you,' he demanded, and pulled a little away from her so that he could see into her face. 'Oh, Elyn, Elyn,' he breathed, his eyes adoring on hers. 'It *is* the same for you, isn't it?'

She smiled, and nodded speechlessly, but it was enough, for with a cry of joy he pulled her close up to him again, and more long moments passed. She felt his lips at her hair; and gently then, Max pulled back to place tenderly loving kisses on her eyes, before oh, so tenderly he placed a warm and loving kiss on her mouth.

'Oh, Max,' she whispered, her heart full of emotion when he leaned back to look at her.

'Dearest Elyn,' he murmured, but then seemed to lose a little of his balance.

'Shall we sit down?' she suggested hurriedly.

'We shall,' he agreed, 'and you can tell me how, when I have been such a devil to you, you have still managed to fall in love with me.' They were sitting snugly together on the settee, one of Max's arms about her shoulders as he held her close to his side when, turning to her, he devoured her face for some seconds, then prompted, 'Are you never going to begin?'

'You're a hard taskmaster,' she teased, wanting to pinch herself to see if this was true. *Was it really happening?* 'But I should have recognised I was in trouble at the absurd delight I felt when I heard your voice at Bergamo airport saying "Hello, Elyn".'

Max was the one to look delighted then. But he wanted more. 'Go on,' he urged.

'What can I tell you?' she asked. 'Should I tell you how, only two days later, we were having a meal—after I'd finished typing a report that was so urgent I had to work late,' she inserted, and loved his unrepentant grin. 'You wretch,' she said lovingly.

'Go on about the meal,' he prompted.

'I looked at you—and was suddenly breathless,' she confessed.

'Because of me?'

'Who else?' she smiled, but went on to confess, 'It was not long afterwards—that same night, in fact—that I realised that I'd done the most unthinkable thing. I'd fallen in love with you.'

'*Amore mia*! You knew *then*?' She nodded, and was soundly hugged, then kissed for her trouble. 'But why unthinkable?' he asked.

'Well, apart from the fact that you were never going to fall in love with me...'

'There, you see, you do not know it all!' he interrupted.

'That's true,' she agreed. 'At first I thought you were an out-and-out philanderer.'

'Oh, my lovely Elyn,' he came in quickly, 'the only reason I took you in my arms that night after our meal was that I simply could not help myself. Always before, I have been in control, but the attraction of you penetrated that control.'

'Honestly?' she questioned, wide-eyed.

'Please believe me—I am just not interested in casual sex, and certainly not with any one of my employees. I prided myself that I had far more control than that. Yet you...' He broke off and gave her a lopsided grin that thrilled her. 'I left you that evening realising that I had better keep out of your way in future.'

'Which you did,' Elyn recalled. 'I didn't see you for an age after that.'

'It was the following Wednesday, to be exact,' he supplied, and Elyn stared at him, her trust in him starting to set hard. She had known it was the following Wednesday—but had he too ticked the days off when they had not seen each other? 'Despite my intention to keep out of your way, it was strange the number of times I found it necessary to walk the corridors near the computer section.'

'Oh, Max, you were looking for me!' she smiled, enchanted, and he left what he was saying for the moment just to feast his eyes on her, and then to place a small kiss on either side of her mouth, before finding her lips and kissing her gently.

'I was hoping to catch sight of you,' he admitted.

'Which you did. I was on my way back from lunch, and...'

'And you, after the briefest of conversations, sailed on by with your nose in the air, and I—I acknowledged for the first time that whatever the emotion in me about you was, it was more than fleeting.'

'Oh!' she sighed, and asked, 'You didn't know then that you—er—loved me?'

'That I love and adore you, *cara mia*,' he corrected, but shook his head. 'I did not know then what this emotion was. All I knew was that I wasn't happy with your cold attitude. Can you wonder,' he asked, 'that I again decided to keep my distance from you?'

'I didn't see you for a whole week after that.'

'You were counting too?' he asked jubilantly, and as she laughed in pleasure at his jubilation, he went on ruefully, 'My darling Elyn, you can have no idea of how you have haunted me. Of how, that next Wednesday, I purposely went to work later than normal, and adjusted my car mirrors so I could sit in the car park and wait and watch for you to go by.'

'It wasn't accidental, that meeting!' she gasped.

'Not accidental at all,' he assured her firmly. 'But when all I wanted to do was to talk to you, I found that I could not be natural with you. Well,' he qualified with a dry smile, 'not until you said you had been sightseeing in Bolzano—when what did I do then but—because you had to have been there with some man—fly into a jealous rage!'

'How wonderful!' Elyn beamed in utter rapture.

'I shall kiss you breathless for that,' Max promised severely, but grinned in pleasure when she laughed happily at the idea. 'However, first things first!' he resumed. 'The next thing that I knew was that Felicita was informing me that you were going away for the weekend with Tino Agosta.'

'We were having separate hotel rooms,' Elyn inserted hastily.

'You were having nothing!' Max told her bluntly, and to her entire amazement added, 'It did not take me long to find a good reason to send him in the opposite direction from Cavalese last weekend.'

'*You* arranged that tutorial!' she gasped, her lovely green eyes huge in her face.

'You are mine, not his!' Max answered with thrilling possessiveness. 'My first thought was to dismiss him at once—but that was before my sense of fairness took over.'

'So you sent him away instead,' she commented, but was startled again when something suddenly occurred to her. 'What an amazing coincidence that you had arranged to go to Cavalese too that weekend, though!'

Max gave her a wry look, then owned, his mouth curving upwards, 'There was nothing coincidental about it, *cara*. I just "happened" to be in the same area as you when you were leaving last Friday night. When I recovered from my annoyance that you, by the sound of it, were still going skiing, I decided it was time I did a little skiing myself.'

'You hadn't intended to...' she gasped.

'I'd no intention at all,' he agreed. 'But it was a simple matter to contact a friend for the loan of his chalet. I drove to Cavalese early on Saturday morning—and from then on spent a most frustrating time looking for you.'

'You were looking for me!'

'I looked everywhere until I became furious that it should matter. I was thoroughly fed up when I decided you must be on Alpe Cermis. But even there I could not find you. Frustrated beyond enduring, I decided that some physical exercise might take you out of my head and took the chair-lift to go higher. And that,' he smiled, 'when I was too high to get off, was when I saw you heading for the trees.'

'You spotted me from the chair-lift?' she asked.

'And fearing that I might never find you again, I had to wait to get off that damned chair-lift before I could come after you.'

'Oh!' she sighed, and recalled, 'And I—I wandered on to the ski-run.'

He shook his head. 'It was I who was in the wrong. But, as I've said, I was anxious to get to you. Anxious,' he said tenderly, 'and loving the concern in your voice when, in my efforts to avoid crashing into you, I swerved too sharply and went over. So much did I love that concern, dear Elyn,' he confessed roguishly, 'that, when there was nothing at all the matter with me, to my own astonishment, I heard myself making believe I was injured.'

'You wretched man!' she exclaimed lovingly.

'It is all true,' he agreed. 'But whatever it was I did not know, what I did know was that I did not want you in some hotel while I was alone in some chalet. But, as we ate our supper and talked, I grew more and more

enchanted with you. Then, my dear sweet wonderful
Elyn, we began to make love, and I was lost.'

Elyn was in a dream world from which she never
wanted to awaken, but as she remembered the way it had
been, she just had to ask, 'Max, was I—er—too—
forward?'

'Too forward?' he enquired, his own expression serious
as he studied her slightly worried face. 'How do you
mean, *cara*?' he asked gently.

Elyn swallowed, but this was no time to hold back.
Max seemed to want her to understand, to have all mis-
understandings out of the way—and so did she. 'When
we were—er—loving each other. I thought, when you—
er—stopped, that it was because I was too easy, too...'
Her voice faded at the incredulous expression that came
to his face.

'*No*!' he exclaimed forcefully. 'It was not for that
reason that I stopped!' he denied. 'Oh, my dear love,
don't you know I was lost—lost to everything, de-
lighting in the warmth, in the naturalness of you? Until
that moment when you said the words "I've never
wanted a man before" I wasn't giving a thought to anything but the beauty we were sharing.'

'My words p-put you off?' she asked hesitantly.

'Oh, Elyn, Elyn!' cried Max, gathering her closer. 'I
was not *put off* at all! I wanted you, with a fierceness
that was driving me crazy. But when you said what you
did, I was reminded that I would be first with you, that
I was about to take your purity—and, while that in no
way lessened the urgent desire I felt for you, I wasn't
otherwise sure how I felt about that. I was unsure about
everything suddenly, and all I could be certain of was
that, by getting you to talk out the pain of your parents
and their eventual break-up, I had made you vulnerable.
Would you hate me in the morning that, vulnerable—
through me—you had given yourself to me.'

'Oh!' she gasped in wonder. 'Oh, Max,' she sighed, and just had to tell him, 'you really are quite wonderful!'

'Speak to me so always,' he smiled, and they kissed and held each other, until, as if determined to get it all said and out of the way, Max confessed, 'I wasn't feeling so very wonderful on Sunday morning.'

'You'd spent the night on that wooden-armed settee,' she recalled.

'That was the least of my problems,' he told her. 'By then you were getting to me in such a big way that in the morning I didn't know where the hell I was. All I knew then was that I still wanted you where I could see you. Against that, I had this almost overwhelming compulsion to take you in my arms—to have you safe in my arms—the whole time. Only I'd done that the night before, and look what had happened.'

'So instead you were distant with me,' Elyn put in.

'And instead of pleasant conversation, we were sharp with each other,' he agreed. 'We went for a drive and I learned, my beloved woman, that because of your fear of debt, you had sold your car. But, even while I was feeling such a tenderness for you for that, you proceeded to astound me by blaming me for the collapse of Pillingers. Do you still blame me?' he gently enquired.

Elyn shook her head. 'The crash had been coming for a long time,' she owned, and, no secrets between them now, 'I'd told Sam repeatedly how bad things were,' she admitted, 'but I should have tried harder. When Hutton's, our major outlet, went bankrupt owing us thousands, and then some of our suppliers refused us credit, we just couldn't hold up. Er—by the way—Guy, my stepbrother, has applied here for work—Hugh Burrell's job, actually.'

'Then we shall have to see that he gets it,' Max promised.

'Oh, Max!' she beamed, loving him so very much. 'Though Guy is brilliant at his job,' she thought to mention.

'All the more reason for us to employ him.' Max smiled, and, seeming to love her happy look, he went further by adding, 'Perhaps, when your stepfather is receptive to speaking with me on such matters, I will discuss with him the possibility of him helping us in a design consultant capacity.'

'Oh, would you?' she asked excitedly.

'I'm sure he has a wealth of experience built up over the years which should not be allowed to go to waste,' Max remarked. 'But, my darling,' he went on, his adoring dark eyes fixed on hers, 'I am, right now, more interested in us than anyone else, and wish you to know how last Sunday in Cavalese I was so emotionally troubled that I was not thinking at all clearly.'

'But you eventually started to think more clearly?'

'It took a fiery green-eyed blonde to hurl a weighty ski-boot across the room at me for me to suddenly realise that, hell take it, I was heart and soul in love with the woman!'

'That was when you knew!'

'It had been there almost from the first, I know that now. But yes, like a blinding light, it was suddenly revealed to me how very much I was in love with you—and how, because you had incapacitated me, I couldn't come after you.'

'I'm sorry, I'm sorry, I'm sorry,' she regretted, and reached up to kiss him shyly.

'Beloved Elyn!' he breathed, and kissed her lingeringly. She was pink-cheeked when he broke his kiss. 'Where was I?' he asked, his voice thick in his throat.

'You're asking *me*?' she choked, her brain away with the fairies.

She loved the sound of his amused laughter. Then, 'Ah, yes,' he remembered, 'So, unable to even hobble, I was eventually stretchered to my home...'

'Oh, Max!' Elyn exclaimed, aghast at the thought that she had been the instrument of all that had happened, 'I'm so, so sorry!'

'You can kiss me better later,' he suggested with a grin, and resumed, 'But at my home, with thoughts of you driving me crazy, I attempted to concentrate on something else by ringing Felicita to cancel my Rome trip and to ask her to bring me some work.' He smiled. 'But you were so much in my head, my love, that before Felicita could get to my home I was putting through a call to you to ask, since I could not come to you, if you would come to me.'

'Oh, darling,' she mourned, 'and I slammed the phone down on you!'

'Did I not say you had a magnificent temper?' he forgave her handsomely. 'I knew then, though, that news of my injury must have reached you—and that you didn't believe it.'

'I didn't,' she owned.

'And who could blame you? However, since it seemed to me that I would only get the same reaction if I attempted to phone you again, I had no option but to wait. By tomorrow you would know everything.'

'Felicita?' Elyn guessed her intelligence at work. 'Since you couldn't put your foot to the floor, you thought Felicita might tell me the next day that you were genuinely injured?'

'There was no "might" about it, sweet Elyn,' he told her. 'I had it all worked out by the time she arrived how she must stress to you the true extent of my injuries, she must tell you how I fell over a ski-boot—and then perhaps, I hoped so much, you would be more receptive when I began to make formal approaches to you.'

Formal approaches? Her heart bumped. It sounded lovely—did he mean, in his wonderful Latin way, when he began to pay court to her? 'Oh, my dear!' she sighed, and was kissed, and adored, before Max pulled back, and again had to force himself to remember what he had been saying.

'Can you imagine my amazement?' he asked, his expression clouding, 'or conceive how stunned I felt, when Felicita arrived and, in reply to my question of how you knew about my "sprained ankle", revealed that you had that morning asked for a transfer back to England! When she said that you had put in your request *before* she told you of my "second" accident, I felt then that I had perhaps hurt you, and that was your reason for wanting to leave Italy.'

'It was,' she owned.

'I shall never knowingly hurt you again,' he vowed, and almost reverently laid a tender kiss on her brow.

'I was also—ahem...' Elyn had to cough before she could bring out the rest of her confession, 'I was also pea-green with jealousy of Felicita.'

'You were jealous!' he beamed, but, astonishment coming to him, 'Of Felicita?'

'I know now that I'd got it all wrong, but—well, I was in a stew about you too, remember, so when Felicita said how you were injured—and I didn't believe that for a moment—and how she was leaving in a few minutes to drive to your home, albeit with some work, I put two and two together and made a neat, if erroneous, five.'

'Because you too have experienced a taste of that dreadful gut-tearing emotion of jealousy, I will forgive you,' he decreed charmingly, but questioned, 'Is that why you ran from Italy without telling anyone where you were going?'

'It wasn't just that,' she admitted. 'I was hurt, jealous, and you'd rejected me, and...' She broke off when his arm instantly tightened about her, and a stream of such emotional Italian left him that she just knew, without comprehending the words, that he was wholeheartedly denying that he had rejected her in any way. 'Anyway,' she resumed with a smile to show him that she was no longer hurt, 'your phone call to me was the last straw. I just couldn't take any more.'

'*Cara*! My beloved,' Max crooned, and kissed her and stroked her face with caring sensitive fingers.

'Oh, my love!' she gasped, and, feeling sorely in need of some humour just then, 'Where was I?' she teased.

'You were flying back to England,' he reminded her. 'Something which it just had not occurred to me that you would do—not before I had begun to pay my respectful attentions to you.'

'Perhaps I do have something of a temper, as you say,' Elyn murmured, and as the thought landed, 'How did you know I'd gone, by the way?'

'How, was easy. Working out why, and consequently hoping, was the difficult part. You'd left the apartment key with the hall porter. He rang my PA the next morning to ask whether he should hold on to it or deliver it to her. Felicita in turn rang Tino Agosta, who assured her that you were never late but weren't in yet, but had gone home early the day before with a migraine.'

'I'd invented a headache,' Elyn confessed.

'You really have to stop telling these lies, Miss Talbot,' Max reprimanded her lovingly.

'Sauce!' she exclaimed, but had to laugh, though she sobered to ask, 'So Felicita knew I'd flown back to England by the time she spoke to you next.'

Max nodded. 'I couldn't believe it at first. You must be exceedingly angry by my deception, I realised. Exceedingly hurt by me too, so hurt in fact that even this fear of debt you have is of no consequence, because, not waiting for a transfer, you had quit your job! By that time it was ten-thirty, Italian time. By ten thirty-five, my brain was racing so fast, and bringing me such amazing possibilities, I could barely remember our Pinwich telephone number.'

'You began to suspect ... You rang *here*?' asked Elyn, trying desperately to keep up with him.

'It was for certain that with my foot the way it was I could not get here in person. Bearing in mind how much you feared penury, it was my intention to speak to Personnel, who were to pass instructions for your salary to continue to be paid into your bank.'

'Good heavens!' Elyn exclaimed in astonishment.

'But I didn't get further than to say I was ringing in connection with Miss Elyn Talbot than I was hearing that, not fifteen minutes ago, you handed in your notice. "Do you mean that Miss Talbot is in work today?" I asked, for I really could not believe it.'

'I—er—Guy, my stepbrother, was upset. He thought I would have the family labelled unreliable, and thereby ruin his prospects of employment with your company, if I just walked out,' she explained.

'Sweet, sweet Elyn, so you did it for him! No matter,' he went on. 'To hear that you were there, to know where you would be Monday to Friday for the next four weeks, was a little solace to me. I had your address, of course, but until today, when I could at last get my feet into two vastly different sizes of shoes—which my good house-keeper purchased on my behalf—I was going nowhere.'

'This is the first day you've been able to get a shoe on of any size?'

'It is—and I've been impatient to get here, to get to you and...' he broke off, looking deeply into her eyes '...and called myself a fool all the way here.'

'You thought you had worked it out wrongly—and that I didn't love you.'

'I've been so beset by doubts, you would not believe it. Then, when I arrived here and got myself together, and when I'd been aching for the sound of your voice, I picked up the phone to speak with you—and was full of doubts again at your sharp tone. It made my tone sharp too.'

'You hadn't meant to speak to me like that?'

'No way! I'd said your name a dozen times. "Elyn, would you like...? Elyn, may I ask...? This is Max, Elyn... Elyn, I have so much to apologise for—would you consider coming to see me", and what do I say...'

'My office, Miss Talbot, *now*,' she laughed.

'Oh, my dear, dear Miss Talbot,' he breathed. 'I love you so very, very much,' and he hauled her into his arms and for ageless moments they kissed and held on to each other. Then Max was pulling back from her, looking down into her flushed face, and telling her tenderly, a husky note in his voice, 'My darling, there is so much with regard to you that I have done wrong that it is important to me that I now do things in a proper manner.' He looked at her long and lovingly, then said, 'So now, my dear, I should like, with your permission, to come with you to see your family.'

'My f-family?' she stammered.

'More particularly, in the absence of your father, your mother,' he explained.

'Oh!' she exclaimed, her wide green eyes going even larger. 'W-well, yes, of course,' she said in a rush, 'I'd be delighted to introduce you to my family, but—but what about your foot?'

'My foot?'

'Will you be able to stand on it?' she asked anxiously. Some of the road up to where she lived was a bit rutted. Even a taxi ride home could prove painful for him.

'I shall stand on it,' he assured her and, fixing his eyes on hers, refused to let her look away. Though she was looking at nowhere but him, indeed her eyes were riveted to his when he stated resolutely, 'I shall make sure I'll be able to stand on it one day next week when I stand and wait for you to come down the church aisle to me.'

'Ch-church aisle!' she exclaimed, her voice a mere thread of sound.

'*Amore mia*,' Max breathed, 'what do you think it is that I've been saying all this while, if it isn't that I want you to be my wife?' Wife! Elyn's heartbeats were all over the place—but suddenly she noticed that there was something akin to a hint of panic in Max's eyes as he insisted, 'You will marry me, Elyn?'

'Oh, my darling!' she cried. Oh, would she not! She smiled, a wonderful joyous smile. 'Er—perhaps we *had* better go and see my mother,' she agreed—and was kissed.

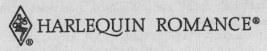

HARLEQUIN ROMANCE®

brings you

Stories that celebrate love, families and children!

Watch for our next Kids & Kisses title in October.

Sullivan's Law
by Amanda Clark
Harlequin Romance #3333

A warm, engaging Romance about people you'll love and a place that evokes rural America at its best. By the author of A Neighborly Affair and Early Harvest.

Jenny Carver is a single parent; she works too hard and worries too much. Her son, Chris, is a typical twelve-year-old—not quite a kid anymore but nowhere near adulthood. He's confused and bored and resentful—and Jenny isn't sure how to handle him. What she decides to do is take him to Tucker's Pond in Maine for the summer—a summer that changes both their lives. Especially when they meet a man named Ben Sullivan....

Available wherever Harlequin books are sold.

Where do you find hot Texas nights, smooth Texas charm and dangerously sexy cowboys?

Crystal Creek reverberates with the exciting rhythm of Texas. Each story features the rugged individuals who live and love in the Lone Star state.

"...Crystal Creek wonderfully evokes the hot days and steamy nights of a small Texas community...impossible to put down until the last page is turned."
—*Romantic Times*

Praise for Bethany Campbell's *The Thunder Rolls*

"Bethany Campbell takes the reader into the minds of her characters so surely...one of the best Crystal Creek books so far. It will be hard to top...."
—*Rendezvous*

"This is the *best* of the Crystal Creek series to date."
—*Affaire de Coeur*

Don't miss the next book in this exciting series. Look for
GENTLE ON MY MIND by BETHANY CAMPBELL

Available in October wherever Harlequin books are sold.

CC-20

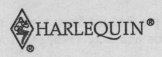

THE VENGEFUL GROOM
Sara Wood

Legend has it that those married in Eternity's chapel are destined for a lifetime of happiness. But happiness isn't what Giovanni wants from marriage—it's revenge!

Ten years ago, Tina's testimony sent Gio to prison—for a crime he didn't commit. *Now* he's back in Eternity and looking for a bride. *Now* Tina is about to learn just how ruthless and disturbingly sensual Gio's brand of vengeance can be.

THE VENGEFUL GROOM, available in October from Harlequin Presents, is the fifth book in Harlequin's new cross-line series, **WEDDINGS, INC.** Be sure to look for the sixth book, **EDGE OF ETERNITY,** by Jasmine Cresswell (Harlequin Intrigue #298), coming in November.

WED5